More Snapshots?
From My
Uneventful Life

T0162975

More Snapshots?
From My
Uneventful Life

David I. Aboulafia

Winchester, UK
Washington, USA

First published by Roundfire Books, 2018
Roundfire Books is an imprint of John Hunt Publishing Ltd., Laurel House, Station Approach,
Alresford, Hants, SO24 9JH, UK
office1@jhpbooks.net
www.johnhuntpublishing.com
www.roundfire-books.com

For distributor details and how to order please visit the 'Ordering' section on our website.

Text copyright: David I. Aboulafia 2017

ISBN: 978 1 78099 374 4
978 1 78099 470 3 (ebook)
Library of Congress Control Number: 2016945827

A CIP catalogue record for this book is available from the British Library.

Design: Stuart Davies

Printed and bound by CPI Group (UK) Ltd, Croydon, CR0 4YY, UK

We operate a distinctive and ethical publishing philosophy in
all areas of our business, from our global network of authors
to production and worldwide distribution.

Contents

Introduction 1

1. Cape *Sway* 5

2. Date Nut Bread 12

3. The Test 18

4. NOT so Merry-Land 22

5. Just a Guy 39

6. Death By *Whatever* 42

7. The Ring 69

8. Max 74

9. Scared *Straight* 81

10. To Sleep, Perchance to *SCREAM* 88

11. After the First Breath... 99

12. Scrooged! 102

13. Who wants to be a Billionaire? 112

To my children, for whom this book was written.
To my grandchildren, who I hope to meet one day.
And to *their* children, who I will never know,
but who, through this small book, may someday know me.

Introduction

OK. You asked for it and now you got it.

Apparently, some of you were bemused, touched, entertained and – dare I say – even *thrilled* by my last attempt at humor and enlightenment, *Snapshots from my Uneventful Life.*

As you may recall, *Snapshots* didn't try to confront anyone with deep and divisive political commentary, or challenge anyone's religious beliefs from the heights of a self-serving pulpit, or shock anyone with vulgarity and explicit exposé. There was no sex, no gore, and no violence of any kind. It wasn't written for the left-leaning or the right-leaning, or for Christians or Muslims or atheists, or environmentalists, or gay people, or straight people, or disabled people, or for any particular kind of people at all.

It was just written for *you*, whoever you are.

And, there were no four-letter words.

How it was able to garner your attention for more than a few moments I really cannot explain.

But, rest assured, I won't make *that* mistake again.

What I'm trying to say is that all in all I tried to stay away from controversial subjects.

OK, so there *was* that one story about driving drunk. Yes, there was that brief account of me rolling a joint while driving down the Long Island Expressway. Well, and yes, there was something about a naked woman in a dormitory. But please recall that I wasn't the one driving drunk. I never *smoked* that joint while driving down that highway and I never laid a *hand* on that innocent woman.

But I diverge.

What I'm *really* trying to say is that I didn't think it was necessary to write about politics, religion, sex or violence in order to be funny. I didn't have to insert a vulgar expletive in every other sentence to be thought provoking. And, I didn't want to *offend* anyone.

You see, by the time I'd written *Snapshots,* I had already dedicated no small portion of my life to offending people. I'd become quite skilled at it over the years, and I found that this aptitude improved considerably when I became a lawyer.

Which, I am sure, is a surprise to exactly *none* of you.

But, for just once, I wanted to avoid doing so. I wanted to write something that most anyone could identify with and I hoped that a lot of people would read it.

These days it just seems so *easy* to offend people. Just slap a profanity laden dance video with writhing, partially dressed women on the old family DVD player and you'll see what I mean. So, there was no sex in *Snapshots:* none at all.

Try to use any of the words Liberal, Muslim, Republican, Democrat, Right-Wing, Left-Wing, Bush, Clinton, Trump, Obamacare, Immigration, Conservative, Abortion, or Taxes in a conversation between three or more people without ultimately offending one of them. You can't; I've tried, believe me. So, there was no talk of religion or politics in *Snapshots.*

By writing *Snapshots* I wanted to speak to *everyone,* no matter what their age, sex, race, religion, politics, persuasion or beliefs might be. I didn't wish to talk to you about divisive subjects and I didn't want to point out any of the differences between us.

Sometimes it seems we'll do just about anything to call attention to our dissimilarities. It's funny how such distinctions have a way of making one person appear *better* than someone else.

Funny, isn't it?

Sometimes, we tend to judge people by accentuating their differences and we do so in millions of ways. We categorize them by virtue of their educational level and economic status, by the neighborhoods they live in and the jobs they have. We seem to love to put *names* to things, and then assign a relative worth to them. Sometimes we seem so intent on flaunting our *differences* that we forget how similar we really are.

You see, that's what *Snapshots* was really about. That's what *More Snapshots?* is about. It's not a unique idea. It's not some kind of lofty, heady concept. I just want to speak to you in a language we can all understand and about one thing that unites us all on a fundamental level, and it is this:

We are the final result of many things but, more than anything, we are a reflection of what we experience in this world. These experiences are embodied in our collective memories, the wellsprings of our knowledge and our beliefs, and where the essence of what we truly are may be found.

But what we call our memories are really only small fragments of our experiences because we can recall so little of our lives. We string our moments of recollection together like links on a chain to make the moving pictures in our minds. These are the *Snapshots* of our lives, the remnants of our living history. Every one of these snapshots is unique, because they come only once, and only from you. But, like leaves on a tree, your snapshots share grand similarities with everyone else's.

This is our common ground. We are united by our common experiences: by the way we process these experiences through our brains, retaining only the smallest portion, and from that fraction forming beliefs, and acting upon those beliefs, and changing others in the process.

Of course, as in *Snapshots*, everything you will read here is completely true, although I concede I have taken a few liberties here and there in this sequel.

Thus, my prior statement, while accurate, is really not, and you may recall there's a word to describe doublespeak like this. It's called *dissembling*.

But, of course, that's *your* word. I call it *good lawyering*.

Anyway, go ahead; read my stories; make my day. Laugh your butt off, shed a tear or two and scratch your head. I want you to do all of these things.

Oh, and yes: I want you to *feel good* after you read this. I want you to be reminded of some of the *good* things in your lives. Don't worry; it'll be easy, because most of my stories end in gay and happy fashion, just like those in *Snapshots* did.

And we all like to feel *good*, don't we?

Maybe we're not so different after all.

Didn't I suggest that already? Perhaps I did.

And maybe I will again.

See you soon.

Cape *Sway*

CAPE MAY, as many of you may know, is a pretty little town in New Jersey, a state known for its football stadium, its pristine shoreline, and its plenary amusement parks. Also, for its miles of liquor stores and chemical plants, and quaint little establishments where you may purchase most any type of sex toy your heart may desire. Or that any other part of your body may require.

But Cape May *is* a pretty little town, really, with its beautiful beach, and its gingerbread houses, and its fine restaurants. And, the classy, oak-paneled bar located at the venerable Congress Hall Hotel just a few blocks from the beach. That's where my wife and I went to have a quick drink before dinner during one of our weekend getaways.

I am not sure how we selected the restaurant, but I do recall that the fare would cost us more than we could possibly afford and that there were five courses of it to be served. This seemed sufficient qualification at the time. But first we decided to indulge ourselves with a harmless, pre-dinner libation.

We entered the hotel at precisely five p.m. one afternoon. Once there, we made our way down a long hallway lined with a variety of stylish shops, to an elegant, u-shaped hardwood bar. Behind the bar was a good-looking bartender in a white shirt and bow tie. Sitting on stools at the left end of the bar were four, 40-or-so-year-old women.

They were drinking. And, they were hysterical laughing. And they became more hysterical as we approached the bar. It was clear that they were trying to communicate *something* to each other, but for the life of me, I was unable to divine just what. To them, it didn't really seem to make a difference, but whatever it was, it was *highly* amusing.

That they were the only patrons in the bar besides my wife and I served to further rivet my attention. I continued to stare at them as I sat on a stool at the center of the bar. The bartender approached.

"What are *they* drinking?" I asked.

"Martinis!" the barkeep cheerfully replied.

"Let's have martinis, then!" I replied just as buoyantly, not bothering to ask my wife's opinion on the matter. To be fair, this is usually unnecessary, as Andrea routinely accepts my scholarly judgment in such affairs.

Soon, a black slate tablet was presented to me with the '*martinis of the day*' listed one after the other upon it in chalk. And there were quite a few of them, too, undoubtedly with exotic names I cannot remember, and each almost certainly containing a secret mixture of liquors and whiskeys now prohibited in seventeen states. So, we ordered martinis, and all I noticed about the drinks at the time was that hers was a muddy brown and mine was a turquoise blue.

As our drinks were served, I heard a *thud*, followed by a high-pitched squeal, followed by a peal of wild laughter. I turned my head and saw that one of the four women to our left had fallen off of her bar stool. Under the circumstances, it was hard to imagine that this had not been anticipated as the natural result of her current endeavors.

One of her drinking buddies sweetly reached down to assist her. But she reached too far, and slid from her stool as if it were coated with duck fat and was unceremoniously introduced to the floor where she joined her companion.

A third woman threw her head back in hysterics at the spectacle, but did so in such a violent manner that she began to teeter backwards on her chair, ultimately grabbing the long hair of the fourth woman to avoid toppling over.

I imagined that would be quite painful, but I didn't have to wait long for confirmation as the woman's stinging screams of agonized hilarity left little to the imagination. She resisted the tugging, of course, and quite enthusiastically, grabbing her own hair with both of her hands in an effort to regain full possession of something she obviously did not wish to part with just yet. But, as she exerted a grand final *heave,* her teetering companion released her hair, and that result was predictable, too: one was permitted to conclude her *teeter,* and the other was thrown backward, her skull making a dull *thump* against the bar.

I motioned to the bartender.

"I was expecting a jazz guitarist," I offered. "But this is fine."

He smiled knowingly. I gulped my blue martini. He watched me drink, closed his eyes, pursed his lips, and nodded his head. I didn't know what the hotel was paying this guy, but it was clear that his working conditions were quite good.

We finished our drinks and we left.

We had one drink each; did I mention that?

OK.

We backtracked our way down the hall and walked by the shops we had passed on our way in. But two things bothered me. It was something about the way the bartender had looked at me. And, it was something about that drink he had served me, but I couldn't quite figure out what it was.

Then, something hanging in a window of one of the little boutiques caught my wife's eye. With an uncharacteristic screech of delight, she propelled herself into the store. I propelled myself after her and this was strange, as well.

Neither Andrea nor I are *shoppers.* I think we're both uncomfortable with the activity and conduct it only when necessary. Then, we seek to get it over as quickly as possible.

And when I *have* to go shopping, I don't wish my wife to accompany me. I don't want to feel like a little kid being dragged around a store by his mother. I don't want my dear bride to tell me to try things on, or to turn this way or that way, or comment on how I look. I really don't want to hear my love say, "You're going to buy that." This is a sentence she sometimes employs with a period and at other times with a question mark, but both uses indicate that it is *she* who will be deciding what I'll be purchasing.

And *I* will certainly *not* escort my wife into a woman's clothing store, mainly because I don't know what do to with myself once I get there. I prefer to stand outside, let my wife peruse the current offerings of the establishment and merely advise me whether my money will be required.

But *that day,* I not only found my wife in such a store – actually *enjoying* herself – but I found myself there as well, gleefully searching the racks, suggesting how hot she might look in this or in that. I was quite vocal about my opinions as I remember, and I also recall not caring what anyone might think of my remarks, which is not as unusual as you may think.

For her part, Andrea appeared delighted by my comments. Her giggling seemed to replay itself as if it were on some kind of continuous loop.

All of a sudden, I realized I'd seized a dress on a rack to maintain my stability. I really didn't think anything of it, at first: meaning that I noted the event without giving it much consideration.

As I walked out of the store, I lost my balance and careened with some force into the entrance door and I noted this, too. The zigzags I proceeded to make down the hallway were also quite discernible.

Andrea thought all this quite hysterical and I agreed, even if we weren't quite sure at the time what *all this* was, exactly.

But, making a long story short, we soon arrived at the restaurant – it was only two blocks away – and a distance we were able to traverse in a mere three-quarters of an hour. I only remember that there was something really *hilarious* about those two blocks.

We sat down at an elegant table, in this truly beautiful place, with our *oh-so-proper* waiter, who described the *unbelievably* sumptuous fare we would delight in that evening.

Which we found *oh-so-friggin'-funny.*

How else can I put it? He announced the specials and we laughed our asses off.

As you may imagine, this was not the response our server had anticipated and it was far from well received. He left in a huff. He soon returned with our salad, and then our appetizers, practically flinging them in front of us and departing in a second and third huff. Clearly, there would be no pleasant banter with our waiter this evening.

We subsequently consumed our first and second courses, which was more food than either of us could tolerate. Then I discovered the room was spinning around me.

I described my state of mind and body to my wife. I didn't really need to, as I had ordered a martini for her as well, and by now she was completely familiar with this state. In short, we were inebriated.

I told her that I "needed to take a walk." This is code in my household and a phrase that is seldom employed. It means, I'm going to take a walk around the block and try to clear my head in the hope I can get through this meal.

I returned after my four-block walk, my head no clearer, and the entire restaurant in the same revolving state it had been when I left it.

The waiter returned with our third course: two pork chops so huge that the end of each chop hung over the side of our plates by two inches. We stared, knowing that at least two animals had to die to make this presentation. We also knew that if we proceeded to dine, other casualties would follow quite naturally.

Put another way, we were not going to survive this. The strange sounds coming from our stomachs were clearly audible – to her, to me, and to many of our fellow diners, I'm sure – and the continual movement of the room that by now had affected us both did nothing to improve matters. We asked for the check, inexplicably requested that the chops be doggie-bagged, and made our exit from the restaurant. We stumbled the block back to our hotel room.

My wife's final contribution to the affair was projectile vomiting. I was thankful that she spared me the singular experience of *witnessing* the spectacle, but this was only because she had the presence of mind to close the bathroom door. However, rest assured that when you hear noises resembling the soundtrack of *Texas Chainsaw Massacre* beyond such a partition, you can safely assume that nothing whatever to do with glee or glad tidings are transpiring within.

"I'm such a *skank*," she said with some embarrassment when she emerged.

I considered this for a moment.

Yes. From where I was sitting, she certainly did take on all the appearance of being a skank.

My last contribution to Cape May was to bequeath our leftover pork chops to the hotel we were staying in, leaving them in our room's mini-refrigerator, mainly because they looked no more appealing in the morning than they had the night before.

For all I know, they're still there.

It wasn't until sometime after our vacation that I finally understood what had happened to us. This revelation came to me as I admired our collection of crystal vases, glassware and keepsakes which are stored in a hutch in our dining room. Among these items are martini glasses in two sizes.

Now this was interesting. I peered closer for an inspection. Six elegant crystal glasses comprised the first set, each glass capable of containing only three or four ounces of liquid.

The glasses in the second set were larger – more of the *partying kind* – and each glass could probably hold six ounces.

I then remembered what had struck me about the drinks at the Congress: it was the *martini glasses* they used, which were *much* larger than those *partying kind* of glasses I had at home.

And then I remembered what a martini is. Traditionally made with gin and vermouth, these days the name is used to describe a variety of drinks that have common characteristics. They may be shaken or stirred with ice, but they are not otherwise diluted by water or soda or anything else. One way or the other, when you order a martini you are ordering pure alcohol and a dizzying combination of spirits to boot.

There were still other facts to consider. *One ounce* of alcohol is usually considered to be *one drink*. It logically followed that *eight* ounces of liquor – or *one* Congress Hall martini – was the equivalent of *eight drinks*, an amount that had already been proven sufficient to cause patrons to topple from their bar stools.

I'm not quite sure why so many of my tales seem to concern *inebriation*. It probably has *something* to do with the fact that alcohol is so readily available. That, and because getting drunk can be so much *fun*.

At least, for the first ten minutes.

Date Nut Bread

IT WAS MY WIFE, I suppose, who started it all, when she brought home this brown, sticky, brain-sized food item, removed it from its plastic enclosure and proudly displayed it, inquiring mischievously, "Does this bring back memories?"

I suppose I should explain.

I don't know how old you have to be to know about date nut bread, whether it is a dim relic of your recorded past, or whether you merely have to be into organic foods, or be a carbohydrate addict, or hopelessly overweight, or a hippy or a Zen Buddhist. Hell, I don't know *who's* supposed to eat date nut bread or how anyone gets to eat it in the first place. I can only tell you that it is a memorable food item for me and one that brings back anything but happy memories.

You see, date nut bread is a food product anomaly. It is not cake and not bread. It's not even like a cinnamon bun or a coffee cake or a carrot cake or anything like that; it's in its own unique category. First, it is probably the only "bread" that once came out of cans. OK, we're going back a few years – to the early seventies, perhaps – but for all I know you might still see a can buried away somewhere, on a forgotten shelf in the A & P where some of the original tins from that ancient time period can no doubt still be found.

Oops. There is no more A & P, is there? No matter. Some of those cans have undoubtedly outlasted the Great Atlantic & Pacific Tea Company itself and will be discovered underneath its ruins sometime in the summer of 2089. With the expiration date still years away.

Anyway...

Even those uninitiated will be able to discern that date nut bread contains dates and nuts. However, also scattered throughout its tempting slices are tiny multi-colored cubes composed of a gel-like substance. I didn't know what these things were made of in 1970 and my understanding has not improved since then. But I can tell you if your date nut bread does *not* contain these things then you are eating a poor imitation of the classic treat. Also, that none of the ingredients can be found in nature or will be listed on any periodic table.

I've already told you that it's brown and sticky. It's also quite *nutmegy,* and a thin slice of it will weigh more than anything you manage to stick in your pockets that day, even if you're a rock collector.

So, as I was saying, in 1970 date nut bread came in cans, and removing this tempting delight from its can was a treat all by itself. First, you couldn't just open the can from one end to remove the product because that would accomplish exactly nothing. The date nut bread would simply sit in the can – content and quite comfortable – and do absolutely nothing on its own to leave. After all, it had probably been there for decades, had made a nice home for itself, and was in no mood to be cruelly evicted by the likes of you or me.

Similarly, little would be accomplished by opening the can from the other end. Date nut bread is very similar to a spoiled child; it will not do anything unless you do it for it. So, if you actually wished to *eat* any, you would have to open the can from both ends and push this mass from one end out of the other. And when you did, the date nut bread would protest with a noise that almost sounded like a human *groan*. It was positively terrifying if you weren't expecting it.

Notwithstanding, I've come to believe that nothing that makes a sound like that can produce any beneficial effect upon the human gastrointestinal system.

What you would be left with would be a cylinder shaped, purportedly edible object that would contain grooves around it left over from the form of the can that contained it. If you touched it, it would stick to your hands, much like flypaper, and was nearly impossible to negotiate.

But Mom found a way.

I suppose that in a mother's mind date bread and cream cheese just *go* together, and this was a truism that was never questioned in my household. It was also universally accepted that this combination of food substances was a perfect substitute for the nutritious, tasty lunch that would typically be served to any vulnerable, tender and growing child on any given day.

Let me reiterate that even in those days few people had ever seen date nut bread. They had never seen anyone sell it, never seen an advertisement where date nut bread was on sale, and certainly never seen anyone eat any with cream cheese smeared all over it. In fact, no one had even heard anyone use the phrase "date nut bread" in a complete sentence. And no one – I mean NO ONE – would serve it to their child for *lunch*.

In those days, every mom made their child lunch before they went to school, because they were homemakers, and that was one of the things homemakers did. I never remember asking my mother to make me anything in particular. There was an established order to things. Mom was La Chef of the kitchen and she decided what to serve me: I ate it or I didn't; that was the extent of my permitted discretion. And with whatever she decided to serve, usually, came the *Scotch Ice*.

Tell me you haven't heard of Scotch Ice?

OK.

For those readers with an interest in ancient history, *Scotch Ice* was the predecessor of those blue *freezer-packs* you have at least *two* of in your freezer, and which are well known to anyone who no longer believes that *frozen water* can cool things.

You start with a small metal can. The outside of the can is adorned with a red and black pattern that somehow makes it "Scottish," but no one can explain exactly why this is so, nor explain what could be *ethnic* about a combination of chemicals placed into a small red and black can which is then frozen. You see, there's a liquid inside the can that, once frozen, will persevere in a glacier-like capacity for hours, and certainly until lunchtime. Thus, "Scotch Ice" became the ideal companion to the date nut bread and cream cheese sandwich in that it kept this oh-so-delicate pseudo-food substance cold.

Mom placed these items into a small paper bag which I was compelled to return with each day because the Scotch Ice had to be returned. I had to carry it with me all day, like an idiot, from class to class. This was another *really cool activity* made necessary when Mom filled my lunch bag with date nut bread and Scotch Ice, and which made me *oh-so-popular* with my classmates, *none* of whom understood what either of these things was in the first place.

In any event, a good tenet to observe when you're preparing lunch for an impressionable child is to never overlook the obvious. It's a good rule to live by, particularly if you'll be preparing him a date nut bread and cream cheese sandwich chilled by Scotch Ice.

The obvious is this: As truly leaden as date nut bread is, it can't stand up to the sheer bulk of a block of ice surrounded by a thick steel enclosure. Its remarkable mass doesn't make it any more invulnerable to destruction than any other spongy, yielding food substance. And the cream cheese does absolutely nothing to improve its invincibility, either; trust me.

So all morning long, as I trudged from one class to another, this soft, pliable mass of flour, cream cheese, nuts and who-knows-what-else would bang and mash itself against the wholly unyielding steel encased ice block known as Scotch Ice. You can only imagine the result but, as I've stated once before in a prior diatribe, imagination is not required. When date nut bread and cream cheese come into contact with Scotch Ice the result is something like a one hundred twenty-five pound accountant making violent contact with a three hundred fifty pound linebacker. Whatever's left after this clash is not a pretty sight, particularly for the accountant. Or the date nut bread, as in this case.

Ultimately, lunchtime would come, like every lunchtime comes anywhere in the world, when little children of every stripe, size and nationality sit down somewhere to dine on the tempting delights their loving parents have prepared for them. One particular snapshot comes to mind...

Most of us had the standard issue paper bags to open; that, at least, was what my lunch had in common with the others. But that was where the commonality ended. All around me, kids were opening up bags filled with Oreo Cookies and Fig Newtons surrounding ham and cheese sandwiches and salami sandwiches and all kinds of sandwiches, none of which was a sandwich composed of date nut bread and cream cheese.

When I peeked inside my bag that afternoon all I saw was the Scotch Ice and a plastic bag containing a gluey, shapeless mass of white and brown dough that looked something like two colors of *Play-Doh* mashed together by the eager hands of a five-year-old. My pitiful repast may have started out as something resembling an edible foodstuff but had responded to the Scotch Ice much like a peanut butter and jelly sandwich struck repeatedly by a sledgehammer.

With some incredulity, I opened the plastic bag in which the remains of my lunch were contained. Demonstrating that inanimate food substances really do have a sense of humor, the vestiges of my meal stuck gleefully to the sides of the bag. I was compelled to pry the two halves of the bag apart to reveal its enticing contents, which separated reluctantly, as if held in place by a combination of bubble gum and Elmer's Glue.

What I saw there upsets me to this day. Although I *knew* what I was looking at – in theory, at least – my brain was having some difficulty processing the information my eyes were sending to it. Whatever it was, it was no longer a sandwich of any kind.

But I was *hungry*. In fact, I was *really* hungry, and the only thing that I had to eat until the end of the day was right before me. Much like a starving man on a desert island, staring at an insect of some sort and wondering if he could actually put it into his mouth, I realized my survival was at stake. I stared at the mess in the plastic bag and it didn't take me long to make a choice.

So I took three fingers and dipped them into that bag as my classmates looked on with amazement and repressed glee. Something with the consistency of melted cheese returned on my fingertips. Those fingertips returned to my mouth – and several times, at that – lending new meaning to the phrase *finger lickin' good*.

The remarkable thing was that it didn't *taste* as bad as it *looked*, but that hardly helped matters, as images of starving Biafran children eating gruel provided by kindly Peace Corps volunteers danced across my mind. Naturally, I couldn't keep this up for very long, as self-hypnosis was a skill that I possessed in only very limited measure back then. I gave up soon enough, my stomach only partially satisfied and my pride demolished, with the sad remains of my feast still clinging to my hands and soon hardening there like newly-poured concrete.

There is no moral to this story and there is little to be learned from it except this; the mind of a parent is not the mind of a child and never shall the twain truly meet. What is completely fine and ordinary to a youngster – like setting off firecrackers in his bedroom, throwing "D" batteries out of an eighteenth floor apartment window, or bringing home the egg casing of a praying mantis that later produces a few dozen flying, buzzing creatures on his windowsill at six in the morning – is abhorrent and fairly inconceivable to any normal parent. Conversely, what appears to an adult to be a tasty and nutritious foodstuff, and perfectly appropriate to serve to a growing child, might seem to that child to be fare better served to an extraterrestrial, and a starving one at that.

The Test

IT IS THE TINIEST OF SNAPSHOTS, an ancient story told by a mother to her son that took only a minute or two to tell, but that I now share with you. It is a true tale, like everything you will read here, and offered as an example of the unintended consequences that can result when we attempt to judge and categorize people.

When I was a child going into first grade, it was not an uncommon practice to have kids take the *IQ Test* so that concerned teachers and hopeful parents could assess their intelligence at a young age. The test purports to be able to expose unique skills, identify learning disabilities and predict behavioral anomalies.

Of course, *all* of these things can be found in me *right now*, and each in relative abundance. Thus, the purpose for testing a five-year-old in order to assign some standardized level of brainpower to him has always eluded me. Knowledge can be taught, more easily to some, less so to others. Usable skills of some kind can be acquired by most of us. All of us can learn and develop and do so at varying times and to varying degrees throughout our lives. What can be gained by such an examination?

I'm fond of saying that if you put a bug under a microscope, you won't see an insect; you'll see a monster. Similarly, if you take any young boy and put *him* under a microscope, there's really no telling what kind of creature will appear on the slide. So, when it comes to kids and the microscope that's the IQ Test, I've concluded that questions answered incorrectly may actually be indicators of high intelligence, an unexpected result that can be conveniently overlooked by eloquent academics, brilliant research analysts and your common, everyday bean counter.

So once upon a time I took such a test, following which my mother received an urgent phone call from the school's guidance counselor. Mom was commanded to personally attend a conference before school officials and to bring me with her. My alarmingly low scores would be the topic of discussion.

Naturally, such an event would be enough to send a cold shiver up and down any parent's spine, and my parent was no exception. Mom immediately broke down in tears and hugged herself, rocking back and forth. She was already convinced that her little boy – who, at the age of four had asked her where shadows came from and why the sun moved across the sky – was in fact mildly retarded and would probably spend his childhood years in some kind of halfway house or group home.

So the conference was held and a lot of people were there. They were all sympathetic and quite solicitous, holding my mother's elbow for support and gently escorting her to her seat as we entered. They all must have looked like doctors charged with the unfortunate task of relating some awful news to a relative of a patient.

Each of them made a brief statement in mournful fashion, nodding their heads up and down in a scholarly manner as they did, and offering their doomsday opinions with great compassion and empathy. I'm sure that their avowals all ended with the assurance that while a keen intellect and a rational mind may not be gifted to all children, even the most intellectually stunted among them will develop *some* brain power: even *me*. In fact, some of these dolts might even aspire to become *garbage men,* who have *wonderful* union contracts, with fringe benefits that are really quite good.

Regrettably, they were willing to demonstrate exactly why they had reached their conclusions.

With that, a kindly, amiable, condescending and patronizing guidance counselor asked me to approach her desk. I elected to humor her and edged closer. On her desk was a blue pamphlet. She turned to an earmarked page and showed me a question from the test I had taken. It was posed alongside a picture depicting a cat with a huge smile on its face, leaping into the backseat of a car. The question was this: "Is this cat happy?"

I, of course, had answered in the negative.

I was asked whether this had been the answer I intended to give. I replied in the affirmative. The counselor looked at my mom with a strained and mournful expression. She smiled sadly and shook her head slowly back and forth as if to suggest, "Mom, I am so sorry, the kid is truly *done*."

The counselor then turned to me. Judging by the look on her face, she appeared to be gazing at some kind of dying lab rat. She asked me to explain my reasoning. She apparently believed that any attempt by me to clarify my disturbed logic would reveal the distressing and deadly nature of my disability, fully support the conclusions of my learned caretakers, and efficiently conclude the conference, save only for a written referral to the appropriate mental health practitioners.

But I was happy to oblige her.

I explained that cats, unlike dogs, were housebound animals. They were not taken for walks. They were not taken off leashes in the park and permitted to run around. They didn't leap into the backseats of cars with big grins on their faces and gleefully stick their heads out of the window as their owners drove away. That's what dogs did. I knew; I had one.

No – Cats stayed at home, and it was logical to conclude that they *liked* to stay at home, since they spent so much of their time there. They would have to be *forced* to leave their homes, particularly if they were going to be made to act like *dogs* who, as everyone knows, are the mortal *enemies* of cats. In short, cats would not leave their homes willingly, and they would certainly not be happy about it if so compelled.

Thus, the answer to the question was *no*. The friggin' cat could not *possibly* be happy.

My mother smiled and sighed, cushioning her heart with her right hand. The guidance counselor's hand was over her chest, as well. But she did not appear to be breathing.

Mom looked around the room. I looked with her. I think we

both wanted to see if everyone there was as stupid as they appeared to be. No one seemed to have anything else to add, so Mom concluded that the conference was over, grabbed my hand and ushered me from the room without a word. The last thing I heard was a female voice behind me: "We'll be in touch!" Of course, they never were.

Twenty-five years later, by the age of thirty, and long before I became a lawyer, I successfully reorganized my first, failing, private school, a task I would repeat several times in the years to come. One of the things I often tried to do was to change the school's grading standards, limiting the weight of traditional examinations and tilting the scale in favor of essays, homework, projects and classroom participation.

Go figure.

Maybe tests are necessary things. Perhaps this world requires – and properly – that we all be assessed in one way or the other. After all, we have to find some way of measuring a person's aptitude. No one would want a doctor confusing their stomach with their spleen, or their lawyer confusing *habeas corpus* with the statute of limitations. I don't know; maybe life itself is just one big test, one that we find out if we passed or failed only at the end.

But to evaluate a child's ability and to *judge* that child are two different things, and we must take great care to ensure that the one does not become the other. We can tell an acorn that it's small, I suppose, but it would be foolish for us to assume it will never become a mighty oak.

We can still ask children all the questions we like, any way we like. But, if we do, we would be well served to keep this thought in mind: that while the answers they provide may tell us something about them, they may reveal more about the adults who posed the questions.

NOT so Merry-Land

OF COURSE, WE WEREN'T *HEADING* TO MARYLAND, my brother and I, when we got into my car for a five day excursion out-of-state. We were going *through* Maryland on our way to Virginia Beach, Virginia, with its boardwalk, and cute shops, and beautiful beach, and hot clubs, and hotter chicks. And, we were celebrating my birthday.

It should have been an uneventful trip, but so many *eventful* things somehow seem to spring from such innocent outings, at least for me. But like so many *uneventful-eventful-events*, this one was merely an extension of an earlier one.

I was at the Limelight in New York City one evening; a lush, decadent club – once infamous, then famous, then infamous again – constructed from what was once an ancient church. And anyone looking at the place from the outside would've thought it *still* was a church: except for the fifty women in micro-miniskirts and revealing blouses waiting outside, in line. All of them appeared to be engaged in animated conversations. Each exchange seemed to pertain to one of three topics: cocaine, alcohol or orgies.

Perhaps you can understand how that might offend some people?

Weird things tended to happen in the Limelight, like when I met this thirty-year-old married woman who told me of the time she asked her husband if he would mind if she slept with two eighteen-year-old boys.

Listen: I'm just telling you what happened. I'm not making any of this up. Think of me as an historian.

OK.

Anyway, I left the club at about 3:00 a.m. – which was late even by my standards – hopped in my car, and turned in the direction of home.

New York City and its surrounding area can be clogged with traffic at most any time of the day, at most any time of the year, but you can usually depend on a smooth ride home if you're hitting the road at three in the morning, so long as it's not New Year's Eve.

Sometimes, however, the traffic patterns are unpredictable. Or as was the case that night, sometimes they can be *preposterous*. Because I made a simple left turn not far from the club and hit a brick wall in the form of a line of cars that stretched an entire city block. As soon as I hit the line, another car pulled up close behind me. Another car pulled up behind that car. I looked over my dashboard. There was about one foot between my bumper and the car in front of me.

I was a rat in a box.

With a lot of other rats, as it turned out, because we all stayed that way, just where we were, for about a half hour. Then we began to crawl – inch by incremental inch – down the length of the street, which was quite a lengthy one as I recall.

As you may imagine, this was enough to fray one's patience at what was now 3:30 a.m.

Some time later this agonizing death march halted, enough for me to see the end of the block just about thirty yards ahead, as well as the traffic light that stood there like some kind of ancient, mechanized sentinel guarding the Holy Grail. It was red, of course, and ten more minutes of observation revealed that this was how long it would stay red before turning an emerald green; a color it would remain in for about seven seconds before turning red again, allowing only a car or two the privilege of leaving this street at any one time.

Every ten minutes.

If you put yourself in my shoes for a moment, you might be able to see how I viewed this as completely unacceptable (don't put yourself in my *head* because *trust me*, you wouldn't like it in there). The traffic light was obviously broken. Only a complete idiot would stand and wait for it. And, for some reason, at this time of night, on this street, there appeared to be a *bounty* of idiots, all patiently waiting on this line. *I* refused to be counted among their number if it could be avoided.

Then, I noticed that there was a cut-out in the curb to my left about fifteen feet ahead. It was a driveway: the entrance to a parking lot that *had* to be empty because it was now *4:00 a.m.* Even if it *wasn't* empty, it was hard to imagine that anyone would have an objection to me using it at this ungodly hour to bail myself out of an equally ungodly predicament. The problem was that fifteen feet of sidewalk stood between me and my freedom, and that distance might take another half hour to traverse. When it would be 4:30 a.m.

Not.

This was one of the simplest decisions I ever had to make, and the fact that my idea might have been slightly illegal was largely irrelevant at the time, though it would become more significant later on.

Anyway, I hesitated not one blessed second before jumping the curb, and I concede it was mildly thrilling to drive those few feet on the sidewalk towards the cutout in the street, although I'm sure it wasn't *nearly* as exciting as when Bruce Willis or Liam Neeson do this in the movies. Then, they always have to drive through several dozen people having lunch at a crowded street-side bistro.

So, I drove down the sidewalk and it was exciting, it really was, and all of the drivers behind me – while appreciating the opportunity to pull up a few more feet – seemed somewhat envious that I had the *cojones* to do something they would never *dream* of doing. Some of them seemed to think I was breaking some kind of *law* or something and began honking their horns in complaint.

"Idiots," I thought to myself.

It occurs to me now as I write that maybe they were *cheering me on,* like prisoners of war watching one of their own try to scale a barbwire fence to freedom.

Anyway, the driveway *did* lead to a parking lot and that lot was *largely* empty of vehicles. As I turned and entered I saw this one car painted an awfully familiar blue and white. As I approached I saw that it contained two of New York City's Finest – commonly referred to as police officers – lurking in their cruiser. One of them was behind the wheel and appeared to be writing diligently: in all probability, not his memoirs. His partner opened the passenger side door, closed it violently and began to advance in my direction. He appeared annoyed and very much so.

The police car was not the only car in the lot. Accompanying it were three other vehicles that had been unceremoniously detained, and that now seemed the subjects of the other officer's writing project. My idea to turn the sidewalk into a roadway seemed considerably less original than it had just a few moments before.

With a motion of his hand, the approaching officer made it quite clear that I was being pulled over, too. Behind me, another driver called out.

"Hey," he said.

This was one of my *compadres,* one of my fellow New Yorkers who had suffered with me through this arduous and painful ordeal in the wee hours of the morning; a brother-in-arms who undoubtedly wished to express his sympathies or, perhaps, even convey his outrage that a peace officer would find offense with a law-abiding citizen seeking only to escape an untenable and unusual circumstance.

I turned my head in the driver's direction.

"Idiot," he said, and then sped away, the now green traffic light miraculously permitting him sufficient time to do so.

I registered my shock at such callousness, but it was hard for me to disagree. I *was* an idiot.

However, when I thought about it, I began to become pretty outraged myself. After all, dozens of cars were being confined to this block all night by a piece of aberrant technology that they were compelled to obey. At any time, these officers might have divined what the problem was and charitably volunteered to direct traffic for an hour or two, which is kind of like *their job.* Instead, they had lain in wait, lingering clandestinely in the lot to nab any wise guy who insisted on getting home before day-break.

I need to add that such conduct is not typical of New York City police officers who, in my experience, have more tranquil temperaments than most if not all of their metropolitan counterparts across the nation. New York is a *big* city, you see, with a *lot* of people and some really *big* problems, and no cop working here typically tries to *seek them out.* This is because so many will come to him naturally – of their own accord, and without any prompting at all – during the course of any day.

But it didn't seem that the officer approaching my vehicle was typical at all. Neither was what he was saying to me. You might say he was articulating his disapproval of my driving habits by employing a diverse collection of expletives to make his point. In short, he was *pissed,* and even if he *was* being disingenuous, my fate was sealed: I was going to receive a summons.

And *that* would have been the end of the matter, except that my sense of outrage grew in proportion to the amount of money the city wished to remove from my pocket as a fine, and the number of points it wished to place on my license as a further penalty.

I did not have to acquiesce to this unfair and wrongful abuse of governmental authority. This was not Red China. It wasn't even Newark. I would challenge the summons at a hearing.

So I checked the box that indicated I was pleading "Not Guilty," put the ticket in an envelope and mailed it away. I am nearly positive that I subsequently received an official communication from the City of New York advising me of a hearing date. I say this with some hesitation, only because things became a little hazy at this point, the main point being that I forgot about the hearing.

I suppose there was a large part of me that knew I'd missed the hearing date. Maybe I thought city officials would just reschedule it or something, or send me a nasty letter. A small part of me hoped I'd just been forgotten; maybe a sheet of paper containing my case had been blown by an errant draft behind a desk, lost forever, except, perhaps, to history. But, mostly, I just forgot about it, and nobody else seemed to care that I had, because that was the last I thought or heard of the affair.

Until.

Until I got in my car to pick my brother up to drive to Virginia Beach. That was when the *Gremlin* spoke to me.

I shouldn't have to tell you who or what this Gremlin is. I've told you many times, in two different books now, and I assume you've all been paying attention.

No? OK; perhaps I'll just quote *myself*, then. I've never done this before and I'm actually glad you've provided me with the opportunity to do so.

The Gremlin is what I call that little voice that speaks to us all sometimes. It's that soft whisper that creeps into your ear every now and then. Call it a second thought, or a second sight, or a nagging feeling, or something that otherwise lies buried in your subconscious, sitting patiently and biding its time, waiting for its moment, a moment when it will be heard.

I hope this clarifies matters and, as I've said, I appreciate the ego boost. Anyway, you should also know that *my* Gremlin is inclined to communicate to me in three-word phrases and did so on this occasion.

Forget the hearing?

I heard what the Gremlin said; I did. I just wasn't sure what it *meant* at the time; I don't know why. I stored its rumination into a small part of my brain, to be digested and considered while I drove to Maryland with my brother to celebrate my birthday.

Of course, as I've stated, when you drive to Virginia from New York, you get to pass through the State of Maryland, where they have state troopers guarding the highways, just as they do in all the states in our Union, I'm sure. I'm also sure that while most troopers are at least mildly concerned about wrongdoers violating their local speed limits, none are quite so concerned as those troopers in the State of Maryland, who get irked over the most negligible difference between your speed and the posted limit.

And that was when the words of my little Gremlin friend came back to me; just as I looked in my side-view mirror and watched that Maryland state trooper approach my vehicle after he pulled me over for speeding. And it must've taken him fifteen minutes to get to me; I mean, I seemed to have a lot of time to consider what the Gremlin had said. It all made sense now and I was surprised I hadn't understood what it had been trying to say earlier.

You see, forgetting to pay a mere parking ticket issued by employees of the City of New York is one thing, but forgetting about a ticket for a *moving violation*, like the one I had, was a different matter. A failure to appropriately resolve a mover could result in the swift suspension of a license.

"Could it be possible?" I asked myself.

"*Naahhh,*" I eagerly replied.

When was that hearing again?

I thought quickly. The trooper was going to ask for my license and run a check on it. I now had to address the significant possibility that my driver's license had been suspended and that the officer would soon learn that it was. Under the present circumstances, I speculated that nothing but unpleasant consequences could result.

Then, I got an idea.

No, you can't! the Gremlin said. It blurted those words out, just like that.

I looked at my brother in the passenger seat. I knew that he was five inches taller than me, with a paler complexion. And yes, it was true that he looked like my mother and I looked like my father. Nevertheless, we were *only* four years apart in age and we did share some common physical features.

I guess.

What if I...

What if I just...

What if I just grabbed my brother's license and presented it to the officer as my own? I was *sure* Mat's license was clean. The cop would just glance at the license anyway and write a ticket – no worries – and then we could get the hell out of here and continue my birthday voyage.

Somewhere, deep inside of me, I heard the Gremlin shrieking.

The officer arrived at my window and bent down to engage me in a brief *repartee*.

There are many times during our lives when we're faced with an important decision. It's true that none of us are soothsayers capable of foretelling the future; none of us can really know the consequences of any of our actions on this planet. However, despite our rank inability to do so, there are some decisions that we just *know* are going to turn out to be bad ones.

Further, some of the decisions we make can be life-changing although we may be unaware of their significance at the time. Sometimes, our choices determine which way we will go in life, and what kind of people we'll eventually turn out to be. This was one of those choices. The thought I had thought of in my head was a highly *illegal* thought, regardless of how expeditious the result might be if it were implemented.

I decided to listen to my inner Gremlin. Its sigh of relief was palpable and quite audible, I assure you, at least somewhere inside my brain.

"Do you know how fast you were going?" the officer asked.

Even as an attorney I have often asked myself whether the answer to this all too common question really matters. It's always an annoying question, and the inquiring officer always seems to believe that this is the first time you have heard such a query; he thinks he is being *original*. And, does it matter whether you *know* you were speeding? You were speeding; you get a ticket. Isn't that how all this works?

In any event, I did know how fast I was going. I was going 62 miles per hour in a 55-mile-per-hour zone. This was slow enough to make any NYC police officer yawn and turn his attention to his jelly donut, but it was apparently fast enough to make a Maryland State Trooper ready the electric chair.

He asked for my license. He walked back to his car. I'm sure there was an incredibly advanced computer there capable of telling him everything about me, including the color of my underwear at that very moment and what I had eaten at the last rest stop.

Somehow, at that moment, I *knew* that my license had been suspended. While I was glad I hadn't given the officer my brother's license, I also knew I'd screwed up and that I hadn't paid sufficient attention to the admonitions of my Gremlin. I was prepared to take my ticket like a man. Undoubtedly, I'd be removed from the driver's seat and my brother would be compelled to complete the journey.

OK; I could handle that.

The officer's subsequent lecture on driving without a valid license in the State of Maryland was illuminating, it was, and I certainly understood why he was so upset. I also understood it when he asked my brother for *his* license. After all, it should've been clear to him by that time that New Yorkers were a crafty, devious bunch that couldn't be trusted for a New York minute, much less a Maryland second. So I wasn't surprised when he confiscated my brother's license and returned to his vehicle to see what color underwear Matt was wearing.

A thought occurred to me. I articulated the thought to my dear brother.

"Is your license OK?"

Silence met my question. Now this was a curious development and certainly not one I had anticipated. I decided to merely repeat the question.

"Matt, is your license OK?"

"I think so," was the response.

I turned my head from my brother to the highway before me. All of a sudden I was overcome by a sense of unreality. Where was I? What was I doing here?

I recalled the answers to these questions as soon as I saw the officer in my rear-view mirror returning to the car. He bent down for another quick chat, just to relay a few more piquing words of guidance.

"Your license is suspended, too," he said to my brother.

Of course it was. I didn't ask my brother how this could be. At that point I didn't think any explanation would improve our situation.

As it was clear that I was on destiny's merry-go-round, I decided that this might be a good time to ask for God's help, so I did. I patiently waited for a response. The officer, ignorant of my request, told us to escort him to the back seat of his patrol car. We dutifully obeyed.

He drove away without a word.

OK. It was clear that God was going to decline to lend any assistance. I fully appreciated that he might be occupied, tinkering around the universe, fully engaged in this or in that.

Then again, maybe this was just over his head.

I asked the trooper if we were being arrested.

"Not exactly," he replied.

Well, that was clear enough. I think my brother and I had intuitively decided not to ask the officer where he was taking us. This might have provided sufficient justification for him to pull over to the side of the road and *cap us* both in the head right then and there. I turned to Matt and whispered in his ear.

"Does Maryland have the death penalty?"

His wild-eyed glare was an adequate response, leading me to believe that it certainly did.

In any event, the trooper kept up a running dialog on the drive to *who-the-hell-knows-where*. I don't remember most of it, but I do remember him asking us this: "You New Yorkers think you can come into the State of Maryland and do anything you want, don't you?"

I believe it was a rhetorical question.

We eventually arrived at a modest farmhouse at the end of a dirt road. He escorted us to the front door. A woman opened the door, led us into a foyer, and called for her husband upstairs.

An elderly man, hair askew, walked down the stairs adjusting his bathrobe as he did. I was told he was a judge. Words were exchanged and papers were signed. We received copies of the papers. I didn't look at them. I was scared *crapless*.

We returned to the trooper's car. His dialogue recommenced. I looked at my brother. It was clear we were *both* scared crapless. I don't think either one of us heard a word the officer was saying. We still didn't know where he was taking us. I stared at the road ahead, which was starting to look a lot like the last mile.

"Clint Eastwood," I said out loud, still staring.

"What?" my brother asked with some incredulity, his lower jaw hanging and his tongue lolling about.

"He was in the movie *Hang 'Em High*," I explained.

"What?" my brother asked again, not enlightened in the least.

"They hang a fourteen-year-old for stealing a horse in that movie."

Matt stopped speaking, but his jaw remained agape. I thought he understood my analogy, and it was this: there was a possibility, at least, that there was no substantive difference between a horse thief and an unlicensed driver in this state. I considered this for a moment.

Nope: I couldn't see any distinction and doubted the trooper would, either.

We soon came to a tollbooth on the northbound side of the highway we had formerly been traveling south on. He told us to wait and left the vehicle. He walked out to the middle of the toll lanes and stood there for a while.

In a few moments a bus – whose sign indicated it was headed for Atlantic City, New Jersey – entered the lane where the officer was standing. He thrust out the palm of his hand as a command – *halt!* – and the bus complied. He wagged his finger at us and we galloped to his side like lost puppies. The bus opened its doors. He pointed. We walked on.

We felt like prisoners being led off to the big house. The bus driver looked at us as if we were terrorists. In sum, we had been detained, transported and deposited on a bus heading back north.

The good news was that the bus ride was completely free. I'm sure the driver was relieved to be rid of us without one of our shoe bombs exploding, thereby placing him posthumously on the front page of the *Atlantic City Tribune* or something.

An additional piece of good news was that we arrived in Atlantic City with thousands of dollars in our pockets. We decided to *go with the flow,* as they say, and make the best out of a bad situation. Hell, we were in *Atlantic City,* after all. So we got a hotel room.

The bad news was that we lost all of our money gambling within two days and found ourselves with just enough cash to buy tickets for another bus that would take us back home.

And, surely *that* would have been the end of the matter, except for the small matter of my vehicle, which had been seized in Maryland. Of course, I also needed to resolve this trifling offense with the Maryland authorities, whoever they were.

I remembered my hearing date this time. It was in some back-water town and it was scheduled for nine in the morning, which was pretty early considering I had a five hour commute. So I left my home, with my brother driving in his car, at four a.m. After a thankfully smooth and uninterrupted trip, we pulled up in front of the courthouse.

Let me assure you that Matthew did not accompany me into the building. He was quite agitated and fully aware that he was in a very dangerous place; he high-tailed it the moment I stepped out of his car.

I was sure that his rapid departure was motivated, in part, by the fact that he was traveling with a wanted fugitive. However, by that time, *I* had resolved my infraction with the City of New York and the suspension on my license had been lifted. *His* license was *still* suspended, and I'm sure *that* had something to do with his anxiety, too.

In any event, I was on my own.

I found my way into my assigned courtroom and waited with a small collection of fellow scofflaws for the judge to be seated on the bench. We didn't have to wait long.

He was an amiable looking gentleman in his early sixties and he appeared to be in an excellent mood, chatting pleasantly with the bailiff and the sundry court personnel as he adjusted the papers before him.

"Lucky break," I thought to myself.

He called the first case. An average enough, pleasant enough looking woman took the stand. She had been ticketed for going ninety miles an hour in a 55-mile-per-hour zone. By all appearances, she was most contrite and understandably so.

The judge's expression underwent a remarkable transformation as he read the woman's case file. His kindly features melted away and his face appeared to warp. Broad lines appeared across his forehead that had not been there before. A dark scowl materialized from nowhere and he spoke, his accent becoming more southern and more guttural.

"Do you know how *faaaahst* you were going?" he asked, glaring at the woman.

"Yes, your Honor," the woman replied.

"You were going *naahhnee* miles an hour in a fifty-five zone," he said, answering his own query quite efficiently. "Do you wish the assistance of an attorney?" he asked.

"No, your Honor," was the submissive reply.

"Do you know that I can put you in jail for a year?"

Now *that* was a disturbing question. The woman reacted accordingly, placing her hand over her heart, making it obvious that she certainly did *not*. Her reaction also made it clear that had she known such a query would be posed she might have shown up in court with Clarence Darrow, Johnny Cochran and *Daniel friggin' Webster* beside her, as I would have if I were in her shoes.

Wasn't I?

The poor lady didn't have an answer to the judge's question. She appeared incapable of speaking at that point anyway and her mouth was certainly open *way* too wide for her to form any coherent words.

"Do you think you'd like to get an attorney *naaw?*" the judge drawled.

She eagerly bobbed her head up and down, like a kid in grade school being asked if she needed to go to the little girl's room.

"Well, go on then," he said, as he set her next appearance date.

"DAVID ABOULAFIA," a bailiff roared from the side of the bench.

I think those were the only two words in the English language that I didn't wish to hear spoken out loud right then. A sharp pain rattled my gut, but a boost of adrenaline powered me to my feet. I approached the bench. This was it.

The first thing I noticed was that the judge's mood had not improved. His drawl was worse than ever.

"Mr. Ahhhboooolayfeeeuh, you've been charged with speeding and with driving in the State of Maryland without a valid driver's license. I see you wish t'call the trooper as a witness?"

"Yes, your Honor," I replied. I had indeed made such a request when I pled not guilty.

In another fourteen years I would actually *be* an attorney and at least marginally capable of cross-examining a witness. But, being a good lawyer is as much about instinct and imagination as anything else and I guess I had that. Besides, I recalled taking at least one college course with the word *law* in it and I had a good idea of how I was going to proceed.

The officer took the stand and was sworn in. I asked if I could approach the witness and the judge allowed it. I didn't learn how to ask that from any textbook: that was just from *television*, but *hell*, I was on a roll already, wasn't I?

I asked the officer why he had stopped me in the first place.

"You wuh speeding," he replied.

I asked him if he had determined I was speeding from a radar gun.

"No," he replied.

I asked him if he had gauged my speed from the speed of his own vehicle .

"Nope, didn't do that either," he said. I turned to the judge.

"Your Honor, I ask that all charges against me be dismissed."

That was bold enough, but I wasn't through, not by a long shot. I continued.

"The officer didn't measure my speed with a radar gun, nor did he do so by comparing my speed to that of his patrol car," I said. "The officer had no cause to pull me over in the first place, his detention of my vehicle was improper and the charges should be thrown out."

For one beautiful moment I thought I was a *genius*. Who needed Daniel Webster?

The judge narrowed his eyes and leaned down from the bench.

"Son, we're not here to discuss whyyyy the officer puuulled yuh ova; we're here to discuss whyyyy you wuh drivin' in the State of Maryland without uh *license.*"

Uhhh, I was dead. I could see that my legal strategy had been based on two small misapprehensions: First, that every legal drama you see on TV is accurate, and second, that the Town of Bumquat, Maryland – population six – cares, one way or the other.

"Do you know I can put you in jail for a year?" the judge asked.

I hadn't, not really, but now I believed he could; I did. He was very convincing.

"Do you wish the assistance of an attorney?" he asked.

I took a moment to glance out of the courtroom window to my right. For some reason, I expected to see a bunch of towns-people constructing a gallows.

I don't know why.

I realized that any further argument was pointless. In fact, any further *anything* was pointless, except giving up. I accessed one final line from my *Court TV* database.

"Your Honor, I throw myself on the mercy of the court." That was about all I had left.

As it turned out, it was enough.

The kindly judge – undoubtedly concerned that I would be unable to feed the town coffers if I were in prison – decided to let me off easy, levying hundreds of dollars of fines instead. I counted off twenties to a clerk, praying I had brought enough, which I had, but barely. Having emptied my wallet, I was now permitted to retrieve my vehicle, which I had not seen in some time and which, had it a mouth to speak and a mind to think, would have been peeved that *it* had to do time in some police lot because of *my* transgression.

My car wouldn't start for two hours. It was the perfect ending to my consummate Merry-Land Experience.

I still go to Virginia, of course, and I still pass through Maryland on the way there.

But with a valid driver's license.

And *slowly*.

Just a Guy

I met Pat one cold day in '94 when my oil burner stopped working.

An oil burner gives you heat. You need it in the winter, you really do. Trust me on this.

My burner broke down frequently and Pat was the guy the landlady called to fix it when it did. He was in his 70s and a tough, hardened, old bird, as so much of his generation was. He also seemed ticked off most of the time. So was I, I guess.

I was usually mad at my landlady simply because she was a not-too-nice person. Pat was usually mad at her, too, but for a completely different reason. Pat was mad because every time he told her what he needed to do to repair the burner she preferred to have Pat "gypsy" the thing instead: apply temporary fixes, rather than permanent repairs.

"Cheap," he said.

This made Pat more money over the long haul, but this also made him angry. I thought that was strange. At first.

Pat knew a lot about oil burners. In fact, he knew *everything* about oil burners, mostly because he had been working on them for half a century. He was an honest, decent, hardworking guy and proud of what he did for a living. He also knew what he was talking about, when he was talking about oil burners. He didn't brag about this knowledge; he knew he wasn't a genius, he wasn't a college grad, he didn't know a lot about a lot of things. He knew about what he knew about and that was about it.

He felt that in a sane world, most people would recognize this and take him at his word. He didn't like that the landlady was cheap and he didn't like that she didn't follow his advice because that was just plain stupid. But what he didn't like most of all was that she didn't let him do his job right.

Pat wasn't a *left wing* type of guy or a *right wing* type of guy.

He really didn't get the distinction. He was just a guy. He loved his country and he had fought for it in WW II, but he didn't think that made him a warmonger. He had learned to hate war and to distrust the people that started wars, but he didn't think that made him a screaming liberal. Pat didn't like the fact that some people cheated the welfare system, but he didn't want to take welfare away from anyone who really needed it. Pat was just the kind of guy who believed there was a right and wrong to things. In a sane world, everyone would understand which was which.

Pat didn't think we were living in a sane world anymore and this made him angry, too. He wondered what had happened to make it this way and he really didn't have an explanation. After all, Pat was just a plumber. He knew oil burners .

Pat and I became great friends. He fixed my burners for the next ten years and then his son did the same for the next five years while he watched. Every time he came over, I stopped what I was doing and we would talk as he worked. He talked a lot about oil burners. I learned the history of oil burners, the mechanics of oil burners, the differences in different models, how to troubleshoot them, maintain them and repair them. I also learned they had personalities.

That surprised me.

Something else surprised me; Pat knew a lot about people. Apparently, they had personalities, too, just like oil burners. They were just less predictable, a little harder to figure out and a lot harder to work with.

Over time, he taught me a lot of things about oil burners, about people, about myself and about one other thing in particular.

He taught me something about anger. Pat knew a lot about that, too. Anger was just a kind of hate, he said. A person who was angry all the time just hated all the time. That hate, over the years, would spread to everything and everybody around you.

Until there would come a time when all that anger and all that hate would have nowhere to go. Then, you'd just wind up hating yourself.

Pat died in Yorktown Heights, NY a few years ago at the age of ninety. I think about him a lot these days because so many people seem to be angry so much of the time. They're angry at bankers, they're angry at politicians, they're angry about health reform, they're angry about unemployment, they're angry about government spending, they're angry about taxes, they're angry about abortion; hell, they're just plain *angry*.

There was a time I'd be angry about some of these things, too. I suppose it's just that now I understand where all that anger ends up.

Pat had disposed of most of his anger by the time he died and he told me so. It had never done very much for him, he said, and there didn't seem much point in keeping it around any longer.

"But what do I know, anyway?" he asked. "I just work on oil burners."

Death By *Whatever*

HOW MANY WAYS CAN YOU DIE? I don't know the answer to this question. I can only say that there's been at least one movie and one TV series on the subject and that I've tried several methods myself. While I don't recommend that you attempt any of them, it is true that living to tell the stories of your brushes with death *can* be amusing.

For others.

It's not that I'm a risk taker, *per se.* I don't have a death wish. I don't climb sheer rock faces or jump out of airplanes for my thrills. I won't go scuba diving or bungee jumping or parasailing. I won't even *watch* The Survivor TV show. Nor, I should add, will I eat any food served from any roadside stand in any foreign country, no matter *how fabulous* the guidebook says it is.

At least, not anymore.

In short, I seek to avoid any activity that either a) carries with it a significant risk of death or mutilation; or b) puts my fate entirely in the hands of someone else. As to the second factor, I seem to have little objection to my *own* stupidity endangering my life. However, I refuse to allow *another* idiot to get me killed, as it's a task I'm fully capable of accomplishing without any assistance whatever.

Notwithstanding, I've often wondered how a relatively conservative and rationally minded person can conduct himself in such a way as to repeatedly bring himself so very close to an untidy and messy demise. These snapshots come to mind...

1. The KEY to Staying Alive

In 1989 I went to Key West, Florida to get away from my wife.

Wait; I don't like the way that came out and it's not quite accurate anyway. Andrea wasn't my wife; she was *almost* my wife. And, I only wanted to get away from her for a *little while*, and then, only to decide whether I wished to *make her* my wife.

Well, at least, that's what I *told her*. I guess if I were to be honest with myself, I'd concede that I did so just to check out a few more chicks before I was *compelled* to be married.

But keep that to yourself, will you?

You see, Andrea was in her early thirties and we'd been dating for over two years. She had reminded me of these two unimpeachable facts on several occasions. And, as Marisa Tomei so famously stated to Joe Pesci in that wonderful comedy *My Cousin Vinny,* Andrea's *biological clock was ticking,* and quite loudly it appeared. It would soon be time for me to fish or cut bait, as they say.

Somewhat in accord with this concept, I thought it appropriate for me to go snorkeling on a barrier reef two miles out in the ocean while visiting the Keys. To get there, I joined about thirty like-minded individuals, boarded a catamaran and headed out to sea.

I like the ocean, OK? I like the pretty little fish under the water, do you understand?

That being said, the ocean is a heartless, unfeeling body of water that will kill you without a moment's thought or hesitation. In my case, however, it sometimes seems to put *quite a bit of thought* into the matter before actually setting out to do so.

So, there we were, thirty idiots with two or three drinks in each of us already, two miles out in the deep, blithely leaping off a boat into a choppy sea. I've never been a great swimmer, but I've always been in decent shape and, despite my relatively small frame, consider myself an athletic type of guy.

I watched as some of my fellow passengers secured life jackets before donning their snorkeling gear, composed of a mask, a snorkel, and rubber fins.

"Amateurs," I sneered, as I jumped overboard with nothing but my equipment, my bathing suit and my oversized ego to accompany me. Then, having hit the water – and not wishing to waste any time attending to the true task at hand – I proceeded to drown, and quite rapidly.

I struggled to swim the whole five yards back to the ladder on the side of the boat and climbed onto the deck. I arrived there, panting, out of breath, shaking my head in disbelief. What had just happened?

Normally my inner Gremlin would have chimed in right then and there with one of its pithy, three-word phrases. It was uncharacteristically silent. So, seeing that nothing had voiced any objection, I leaped back into the water for another try. And, in thirty more seconds I found myself back on the boat's deck, in much the same condition as I had been just moments before.

There's an undercurrent, the Gremlin explained impatiently, breaking its silence and undoubtedly shaking *its* head at my ignorance.

"Oh; OK, thanks," I replied to myself, immediately realizing that *I* was using three-word phrases just like *myself* just had. So, clinging to the deeply idealistic notion that my life still mattered, I requisitioned a life jacket, abandoned my self-esteem and sense of self-worth on the catamaran and took my leap of faith for the third time.

And it was fine, it really was. The water was choppy, to be sure, but the view underwater was nothing short of spectacular. Fish and sea creatures of every imaginable color and stripe abounded there and I found myself overwhelmed and delighted by the sights. I remained underwater, breathing through my long plastic tube, for just over five minutes.

I have related to you, in my previous manuscript, my admittedly cynical belief that a life jacket's sole purpose is to facilitate the job of rescuers by ensuring that dead bodies remain floating on the surface of the water long enough to be expediently retrieved and disposed of. Now you'll learn how and why I initially formed this opinion.

When my head finally burst out from beneath the sea, the

first thing I saw was a little boat about the size of my thumb floating on the water. Which I thought was strange. I certainly wasn't in my bathtub and in any event it had been 25 years since I had been eight years old.

Be that as it may, I quickly realized that what I saw before my eyes was not a child's toy, but the vessel I had leaped from just minutes ago. It was now a dot on the horizon, an afterthought of a ship, an illusion, a mirage, a tiny, itty-bitty little *speck* out there in the depths of the ocean that couldn't possibly be as far away as it seemed.

But it was. One sentence immediately floated across my mind.

"If you panic, you will die."

My Gremlin sat somewhere in my brain, in a huff, peeved that I'd beaten it to the punch with a terse one-liner and also annoyed that I hadn't confined myself to using a three-word phrase as it did when it chose to communicate.

Apparently, I'd broken some kind of *rule* or something.

The next moment, a truly imposing eight-foot wave crashed over my head, filling my tube with water, making it useless as a breathing device. I choked and ripped it from my mouth. My impending demise was right there in front of me. And beneath me, and over me, and all around me.

I have previously asserted – and in self-serving fashion, I'm sure – that I carry with me the potential for spectacular heroics, as many of us do. However, such stout gallantry is usually exercised for the benefit of others, not I. In truth, this is much easier to accomplish than it sounds, mainly because the consequences of failure – as often occurs – will in such event be borne exclusively by those *others*.

Now, however, the penalty for failure was *death – MY DEATH* – and the resulting sentence promised to be carried out with swift reliability. So, as heroes often do, I thought quickly and acted automatically.

What I'm really saying is, there wasn't enough time to call a *meeting* or anything. Nor did I have the opportunity to ask the audience or phone a friend.

I reasoned – counter-intuitively – that an open plastic tube leading to my mouth with waves crashing over me was now more of a dangerous burden than anything. So, I abandoned it to the ocean. I took a deep breath and dove underwater, where the crashing waves of the open sea would not affect me. I swam slowly and steadily, stabbing my head above the surface every thirty seconds or so to take another breath and check my bearings.

As I gradually made my way back in the direction of the catamaran, I struggled not only against the ocean, but to push a very disturbing thought from my mind. Believe it or not, I did *not* consider whether I might be consumed by some sea creature as I attempted to make my way back to the ship. Let me explain…

I'm sure that many of you have seen the movie *Jaws*, that truly terrifying Steven Spielberg production, where a massive great white shark dines – repeatedly and with atrocious table manners – on beachgoers who are enjoying the fun and sun in a New England resort town.

Well, in 1979, that groundbreaking film was only a few years old and still fresh in everyone's mind. Within a year of its release it had already been credited with causing a nationwide fear of sharks and reducing beach attendance anywhere there *was* a beach.

The point is, had I allowed myself to think of *that* cinematic triumph, I would have been more inclined to give myself up to the sea and *allow* myself to drown. Moreover, I would've done so eagerly rather than engender any pitiful attempt at self-rescue and risk winding up as little more than a meager appetizer for some multi-toothed nightmare residing beneath the waves.

Anyway, notwithstanding that I was a pitiable swimmer, and despite the fact that I was – say – *thirty jillion miles* away from the boat, the *really* disquieting thought I had was that no one on the boat knew where I was. Or *who* I was. Hell, everyone on the vessel was so drunk they didn't know who *they* were. And, it wasn't exactly like they'd done a *head count* or anything. That damn ship could easily take off without me and the only person who would have any idea that something might have happened to me would be that guy on the dock in Key West who I'd rented the underwater camera from. And it had looked like *he* only understood *Korean*.

You won't survive, the Gremlin stated, and quite cynically, I thought. It was clear to me that it was dismally unaware that if *I* went down with the ship – or, more accurately, *without it* – that it, too, would be lost to the sea.

Wouldn't it?

But do not despair, Dear Readers, for once again I've set you up for a happy ending (OK, I get it; you saw it coming).

Discipline, my friends, is the most important quality anyone can have, or so I have come to believe. I've oftentimes said that only those who lose their heads are lost, and you may certainly quote me in this regard. I am happy to report that I kept mine and made slow but steady progress, stroke by painful stroke, back to the ship. When I arrived there – exhausted but relieved – they were pulling bloodied snorkelers one by one from the water.

You heard me. In my absence, a school of barracudas had stopped by for a bite. Literally.

Have you ever seen a barracuda? I did once, up close, while snorkeling off St. John Island. They're about six feet long full grown, with one of those six feet being a mouth filled with razor sharp teeth. Their eyes are memorable. Cold and pitiless, they give the impression they're really *upset* most of the time. And hungry, too.

But barracudas won't *eat* you, not exactly; perhaps it is that humans don't taste very good without a side of seaweed and a little *Dijon mustard*; I don't know. But I assure you they are aggressive creatures and will most happily rip you to shreds for no reason whatsoever. And certainly without the formality of any written notice prior thereto.

Anyway, the first time I saw one of these charming creatures I learned something. No, silly; I didn't learn to *stay out of the water*. *That* would have made me *intelligent*. Nor did I learn to snorkel with a spear gun, or wear a *Kevlar* vest or do so in a shark cage, or acquire any other such useful tidbits of knowledge.

No. What I *did* learn was that if you announce your astonishment at seeing such a fish underwater, and upon doing so employ a phrase that begins with "Oh," and ends with a four-letter expletive, you can actually *hear* yourself speak it underwater.

That was a revelation.

Anyway, I lived to tell so much of my Key West adventure as contained in those snapshots of my uneventful life, the subject of this tale, as you have all effortlessly surmised by now.

One would've thought this bit of excitement sufficient for even such a reckless individual as myself, and certainly enough thrills for one vacation. But this was not the case. Fresh from my adventures at sea, I decided to shoot north for a little visit to the Everglades, one of my favorite places in the world. It's an excellent place to tempt fate. Because in the Everglades, much like in the open sea, it is always *something's* dinner time, and there are a multitude of creatures who look at you as just another one of those varied food items their nutritionists are always *bugging* them to eat.

2. BUG-Oblivion!

When one drives down the sixty-odd-mile road leading through the Glades, the first man-made structure you come to is an elevated boardwalk that extends about 100 yards into the marshland. If you stroll to the end of this walkway and look over the bayou, you'll typically see nothing but wetlands.

But on this particular day, as I pulled my car to the side of the road and walked down the wooden path just to see what I could see, what I saw was a cloud of smoke at the end of it. Which was strange, since there didn't appear to be a fire of any kind. More so, the smoke did not seem to dissipate at all as I got closer. So, predictably, I walked even closer for a better view.

Now many people are afraid of bugs, but most people are simply *annoyed* by flies. They're filthy little things that buzz around your head, step in your food and, all-in-all, are pretty high up on the *repulsive* scale as far as creepy-crawly things go. But then there are *horseflies.* Horseflies – which any country dweller is familiar with and which most city folk are unfamiliar with – are much *larger* than your ordinary housefly, although they're fully equipped to achieve all the things your typical housefly might aspire to. And, while they look much like any old fly would – if placed under a magnifying glass – they do have a few distinguishing characteristics.

First, in addition to being *huge,* they're also *bold*, and display a noticeable disinclination to be shooed away by any mere wave of the hand. In fact, such an action actually seems to *turn them on.*

Second, while they have little problem traveling around lone wolf style, unaccompanied by any of their close friends or relatives, they're not at all averse to the occasional family reunion. Given the right conditions they can throw quite a *wing-ding,* if you know what I mean.

Oh, and one other thing. They bite you and drink your blood; did I mention that?

Oh. I didn't. OK.

So, I was looking at this strange cloud of black smoke when all of a sudden I heard a clanging sound, which was jolting and weird, because I was all alone in the middle of the jungle. It took a moment for me to realize that it was only the Gremlin ringing a dinner bell inside my head.

Which, of course, was fully audible to the dark cloud of horseflies I had confused with the aftermath of a campfire.

All twelve *quadrillion* of the horseflies.

My eyes bugged out – which was certainly appropriate under the circumstances – and I began to slowly edge backward. Each fly turned its disgusting black head in my direction which, owing to the sheer size of them, I was able to see quite clearly. Then they started to advance in my direction. *All* of them, and all of them at the same time. At which point, I determined that *edging* backward was a bit too leisurely a pace given the present state of affairs.

I turned and I ran like hell back to the safety of my car, slammed the door shut, made sure all the windows were closed, took a deep breath and wiped the cold sweat from my brow with my forearm.

"*That* was *close*," I said to myself, or to the Gremlin, or to both of us, chuckling darkly as I did, realizing that I had just high-tailed it about 100 feet because of a flock of *bugs.*

I also realized that it wasn't the first time I'd been compelled to do so. Years before, I'd been obliged to jump from the second story window of a deserted building I was exploring with a friend. As we entered one particular room, he kicked a heap of clothing lying on the floor, which he'd mistaken for a dead body. He realized his error when the hornets nesting underneath the pile expressed their disapproval, and with a certain enthusiasm.

Of course, then, there were only about *three quadrillion* hornets. And there was not one vampire among them.

So, there I was in the Glades, sitting in my car, when I began to hear something like hail rattle against my rear windshield. I looked up and out of my front windshield at what appeared to still be a gloriously sunny day. I looked in my rear-view mirror to see the equivalent of black pebbles striking the glass behind me.

You're being attacked, the Gremlin suggested.

"Am I?" I asked myself.

I believe so, the Gremlin replied, with uncharacteristic hesitancy. I think even *it* was surprised.

"Is that possible?" I spoke out loud to no one at all.

The Gremlin certainly didn't need to respond – and it didn't – as it had already answered the question. Besides, reality spoke quite clearly all by itself.

The horseflies – apparently in a feeding frenzy – and displaying all of the delightful attributes of suicide bombers – were propelling themselves against my vehicle in an attempt to get in.

More accurately, in an attempt to get *me*.

I wondered how much blood a man might lose after being attacked by a herd of horseflies.

I wondered how much blood a man needed in the first place.

Not being equipped to provide cogent responses to these queries, I elected to simply further my previously conceived strategy. Which was to flee for my life.

So I hit the gas and took off. And so did the horseflies.

I concede that in my practice as a litigator I have, on rare occasion, referred to one of my dear colleagues at the bar as a bloodsucker. I further admit I intended no compliment by the remark. So, understanding that many of us have as much an aversion to lawyers as we may to bugs, I surmise that a *bloodsucking bug* would be something most of us would really wish to avoid.

But it's one thing to merely *dislike* something and another thing to be *hunted* by that something. Or, as in this case, twelve quadrillion somethings intent on consuming me.

I assumed at the time – and reasonably, I thought – that I might lose the insects at 25 miles an hour or so, but this was not the case. I watched them chase me in my rear-view as I drove. I was quite amazed at the spectacle, as well as how *famished* they all seemed to be. Actually, I was astonished that they were big enough to *see*. I scratched my head and wondered how long they could fly this way.

With my eyes glued to the mirror, I also tried to remember if I had gassed up at the last rest stop.

When my vehicle reached 35 miles per hour, most of the hoard slipped away out of sight. But one crackerjack remained, a big, black, vibrating dot I could clearly see in my mirror, trailing my car at a distance of only a foot or two.

But sixty miles is a challenging distance even for the king of the horseflies to travel. After a few minutes of 40 miles per, I left my adversary in the dust.

"**** *you*," I said at the mirror, to the horsefly.

I'm not proud of it, but I said that; I did.

Now realizing that I had cheated death twice already on this little get-away, I decided that a bit more prudence was probably advisable. I drove for another hour without stopping until the road ended. I parked in a deserted dirt lot and, wishing to be a tad more cautious, sat in my car for ten minutes just to make sure I wasn't being followed, and that this wasn't some kind of subterfuge those horseflies had carried out many times before, on a thousand unsuspecting tourists.

Ultimately assuaged, I left my car, walked a few yards from the lot and found myself on a small deserted beach overlooking a lagoon. The scene was quite beautiful, restful, peaceful and serene. Which was the exact prescription required at the time for a young man who had just spent the last two days swimming, running and driving for his life. Truth be told, I was exhausted from the effort. After a few moments, I found myself drifting off to sleep.

Freeze Frame:

Some of my tales – and this one in particular – concern that little beast that I call the Gremlin, and it occurs to me that some of you out there don't believe it exists at all, and probably find it outlandish that I would think that you do.

Still others – while prepared to accept *in theory* that we all have a nagging sense of *something* pulling at our brains once in a while – regardless of the name we put to it – find it difficult to believe that *my* Gremlin actually *speaks,* and in *sentences,* no less.

Finally, even those who *believe* in the Gremlin, and who *believe* that it can speak, *and* in sentences, simply cannot accept as true that it does so exclusively using three-word phrases.

All I can say is this: you're entitled to your opinion. I'm not making this up and I didn't put the little sucker in my brain. I don't tell it when to speak or how to speak or what to say. It just says and does what it wants, whenever it wants, just as my children have done for over two decades, and just as my poodle does every day of his life. So, *I* don't find any of this unusual or *disbelievable* at all. In fact, I'm surrounded by an entire *world* of *disbelievable* things.

Over the years, I've become quite accustomed to it all.

In any event, I make this explanation only because the Gremlin was extremely active on this vacation – and for obvious reasons, I think – and I just wanted to make sure you were still *with* me on this.

You're not. Oh. OK.

3. *See you GATOR*

Picking up where I left off: after a few moments on this beautiful little beach beside this peaceful and serene lagoon, I found myself drifting off to sleep. And, as I've stated at least once before, I would have drifted quite a distance were it not for the Gremlin.

Open your eyes, it said.

Now there's really no way to turn the Gremlin *off*, you see. It's not like you can flip its *switch* or anything like that, not even by falling asleep. And, not only can I not stop it *speaking*, I can't keep myself from *hearing* what it says, either.

But that doesn't mean I always *do* as it says, at least not right away. This time, even though I was asleep, I took the opportunity to consider the Gremlin's words carefully.

"Why would it say that?" I asked myself in my sleep.

Then, I considered a little more.

"What was that I saw just before I drifted off to...?"

Well, I *had* seen *something* distinctive, something unusual, something a bit out of the ordinary. I just couldn't remember what it was.

Remember the sign? the Gremlin hinted, clearly losing its patience and obviously peeved that it had to spell things out for me.

I thought for another moment. And then I remembered.

"I do!" I exclaimed to myself, now quite proud that I'd figured all this out in my sleep, with only the slightest assistance from my pixie-like companion.

"What did it say?" I asked the Gremlin directly.

I only remembered – and only then – that it was a very *large* sign: that it was posted right at the waterfront: and that it contained bold-faced words written in bright red lettering.

Recall initial advice, was all the Gremlin had left to say.

So, once again, and as I've done throughout my life, I followed the Gremlin's guidance and opened my eyes.

There was a sign, all right, only it was *much* larger than I remembered. All of the words were in great big, bold-faced capital letters. And the letters on the sign were not just *red,* but *really* red, a bright, fire-engine red that no one could overlook or disregard. Even though I already had.

This is what the sign said:

<u>CAUTION</u>
ALLIGATORS COME ONTO BEACH

Well, that was clear enough.

You see, in the Everglades, of all the creatures that will look at you as just another selection on the *prix fixe* menu for the day, none are more well-known, more dangerous, more frightening, or more *friggin' plentiful* than the alligators. They practically epitomize this great national sanctuary and they can be seen in relative abundance.

Hell, they're *famous,* so they certainly don't have to herald their presence with bright red billboards. They don't even have *agents* or anything.

Now you do have to *look* for them, but only because they blend in so perfectly with their natural surroundings. But, let me assure you, they're not hiding from you in any way. In fact, they don't care whether you see them or not, or care about much of anything, except how easily you'll slide down their gullets. *After* they have a bit of *fun* with you, of course. They truly are the court jesters of the animal kingdom, as anyone who has seen one of these charming beasts attack and consume a wildebeest on a National Geographic special can attest.

It was a remarkable experience for me to open my eyes; to have them slowly focus upon that sign; to have the meaning of the words on that placard slowly sink into my brain and for me to realize that I was a mere ten feet from the water's edge.

I allowed myself a few seconds to look at the sign, then at the water, then at my feet, then at the sign, then at my feet again. I wound up *staring* at my feet for longer than I should have. I guess I was amazed they were still there and still attached to the rest of me.

Then, adrenaline poured into my system as if it were surging from a fire hose. I not only leaped to my feet, I leaped three feet into the *air.* I seemed to hover there, suspended, my body abjectly refusing to abide by the laws of gravity and return to earth, only because it seemed so *dangerous* down there.

Such a shmuck, the Gremlin said.

OK, it didn't really say that. That's the first thing I've made up. I apologize and I take it back.

It just *sounded* funny.

In any event, and once again, my recklessness and shortsightedness had put my life in danger. Once again, that annoying little sprite residing in my head had saved me from myself.

But *no* ladies and gentlemen, boys and girls, I wasn't through yet; possibly because I was still alive and hadn't finished what I'd set out to do. Which was to terminate myself in the most horrific way possible.

So, undeterred, I turned from the beach and walked into the jungle.

4. A Bungle in the Jungle

As I've stated, the main road into the Everglades lasts for about sixty miles, after which all that remains is a tropical forest. Although the Glades is surely a tourist destination, this is no Disneyland. Man has put his stamp on this great natural setting just so much, after which he has been content to leave it just as it is and has always been.

Where that road ends, civilization ends as well, and something completely different begins. You won't find any neatly manicured paths, or cute little signs that explain everything you're seeing. There are no guidebooks or pamphlets being distributed by friendly park rangers. There are no jitneys to ride around in while you enjoy the sights, as appealing All-American teenagers with perpetual smiles on their faces speak into microphones and gently urge you to keep your hands inside of the vehicle.

Nor will you find Donald Duck or Mickey Mouse. *They* can be found a few hundred miles north in Orlando. Perhaps these famous creatures *were* here at some time; hell, I don't know. But if they were, they were definitely consumed by something or other long ago. And, undoubtedly, mere moments after their arrival.

Bear with me for a moment...

As you may have realized by now, I'm no stranger to the outdoors. I go snorkeling, take long hikes and, arguably, engage in rock climbing. I've looked death straight in the face several times during these excursions. I'm tempted to say that my recklessness has been too excessive for me to describe, and that these life-threatening episodes are too numerous to list. But it isn't and they aren't, and I am anything but disingenuous, so here goes.

In Jade Cove, California, standing on a one-foot-wide path, with my back to a sheer rock wall, eighty feet above a rocky beach, I lost my balance and nearly fell to my death attempting to take a picture of the scenery.

In Monterey, while scaling a dozen connected rocky outgrowths that protruded a quarter mile out to sea, I almost plunged from a height of fifty feet while taking a *selfie*. While *I* nearly expired, the picture of me almost toppling into the sea was never in any danger at all and made for a wonderful vacation memory.

It is my habit to not only document each ascent with a photo of myself, but to never go *down* something the same way I go *up*. This makes for *variety*, I suppose, and a more intriguing climb, but it does tend to create a few surprises every now and then. As I descended one of the crags in Monterey – still shaking from my near-death experience just moments before – I reached the bottom of one rock to the point where it met the sea and realized that from my vantage point there was no way to get to the next boulder. I had to try a different route, but quickly discovered that what goes down is not necessarily permitted to go back up. The rock wall I had descended was just a bit *moist*, as you may imagine, and covered with sea slime of one kind or another, which made scaling back up quite impossible.

I hung there, clinging to the rock like an idiot. A sea lion watched me as I struggled. At first I thought it was laughing at me. Then, I could swear I saw it licking its lips. I thought *that* was strange.

Aren't they *vegetarians*, or something?

I was saved only by a small miracle of topography. I found myself able to move horizontally across the mount for about ten yards, coming across handholds on the rock that seemed to be placed there only for my convenience, proving not only that God works in mysterious ways, but that He can be found in the most unlikely of places.

I was repeatedly attacked by a rattlesnake in Montauk, New York, as I blithely subjected the animal to a photo shoot as if it were a cover girl, foolishly failing to gain the creature's permission prior to doing so, and oblivious to the fact that I was probably risking my life.

Hiking in the Catskill Mountains, the Gremlin abruptly grabbed my shoulder, causing me to freeze in mid-step with my foot hovering above a coiled copperhead snake. It was only waiting – and quite serenely – for me to complete my stride. While this demonstrates that patience is a virtue, and that even a beast can possess it, I am certain that had I completed that step, the beast's tolerance would have quickly expired, after which time it would have undoubtedly expressed its displeasure in the most unambiguous of ways. Thereby causing *me* to expire.

At the time, I believed even the Gremlin was too petrified to speak.

Snorkeling off the island of St. Maarten with my two, adorable, then teenage daughters, I came upon a deserted beach littered with incredibly beautiful, multi-colored stones, the likes of which I had never seen. Nearly all of them weighed about five pounds each and were about the size of my hand. I *had* to take some back with me.

I *had* to. Do any of you understand this?

I took one rock and placed it in the left pocket of my bathing suit. I took another and put it in my right. I seized one stone in my left hand and one more in my right. It never occurred to this thrice-degreed simpleton that it would be more difficult to swim in this manner.

Do any of you understand *that*?

I didn't think so. But, perhaps you *will* understand an adage I'm fond of repeating to myself now and again: that I became a bit more stupid with each college degree I acquired. Had I obtained one more, I likely would've become a *complete* imbecile.

As I re-entered the water, for some bizarre reason a series of news clips and film scenes began to flash randomly across the movie screen that is my mind. Each had something to do with the disposal of bodies in water.

They would be weighted down with chains. They would be weighted down by feet cast in blocks of concrete. They would be weighted down with an anchor, or placed in a heavy barrel. In short, they would be *weighted down*.

Oh, and yes: sometimes the bodies would be weighted down with *rocks in their pockets*.

Hmmmm.

In moments, triumphs of the silver screen were the very least of my concerns. Just yards off the beachhead a considerable wave ambled by, flooding my breathing tube and nearly dashing me upon some boulders located there with some precision by a deity who, as generous as He had been on prior occasions, had now lost his temper along with his patience and felt that I needed to be taught a quick lesson about *idiocy*.

I struggled back to the sand, choking, coughing and gasping for breath, my chest on fire.

My girls watched me as I struggled with a look of wry amusement on their faces. *They* didn't need any rock samples, nor did they see fit to follow me when I dove back into the water. Neither of them had earned their college degrees by that time, and they suffered from none of the mental disabilities that had burdened me along with my mini-boulders. They knew their dad would promptly return to that beach, one way or the other, dead or alive, and I didn't keep them waiting long at all.

Still finding it difficult to breathe, I told them to return to their mother and leave me to fend for myself. Clearly annoyed by this time, they did as they were instructed.

My children have often accompanied me on excursions such as these – into ocean, mountain and forest – since they have each been five years old. As can be seen, some of these adventures have been quite hazardous.

For *me*, that is. *They* have never been in any real danger at all, mainly because they have religiously followed the one rule I've set as a precondition to their participation; they must do exactly what I say, exactly when I say it. They have taken this advice to heart and they've survived quite nicely.

I suppose it's been a great deal for them. They are required to obey my commands for only a few hours, after which time, they are not. I guess you could say it's really *their* rule that I follow; If I want them to accompany me to these places, these places are the *only* places in which they will listen to anything at all I have to say.

For the last eighteen years or so, I've complied with little resistance.

My wife, of course, being of sound mind, and wishing to remain of sound body, never accompanies us on these escapades. She is content in her role as the *surviving* spouse. After all, *someone* has to call the ambulance, and *someone* has to fill out the missing persons report.

Andrea calmly waits for us in our car, or in our hotel room, or on a beach, as was the case in St. Maarten, often reading a novel as she passes the time. She functions much as an alarm clock does in this regard. When I hear helicopters whirring above me, or bloodhounds barking, or Coast Guard ensigns shouting my name through a bullhorn from the deck of a ship, I realize we've stayed out too long.

Of course, as you may have guessed, I did return to my family in one piece that day, and with most of my little pebbles, too, although I was really *pissed* that at one point along the way I was forced to choose between one of the rocks I was holding and keeping myself afloat a while longer.

I add only that the $400 cash and credit card – which I had wisely secured in a plastic bag in the rear pocket of my suit – were also unfortunate casualties of this experience, demonstrating that risking your life can not only be *dangerous* but *expensive,* as well. I was comforted only by the thought that some impoverished sea creature would now be able to treat his spouse to a *truly spectacular* anniversary dinner.

In New Paltz, New York, while staying at the venerable Mohonk Mountain House Resort, my daughters and I commenced a 300-foot climb that started out as little more than a difficult hike on a defined trail. It ended with a terrifying 75-foot ascent up a one-foot-wide ladder that was positioned in the center of a gigantic crevice, in a mountain peak which narrowed as we advanced. The ladder terminated at a three-foot-wide hole that opened to the top of the mount. My girls scrambled out and through the gap with little trouble, but I found I was unable to follow. I managed to get to the top rung of the ladder, and thrust my cranium through the opening. For some reason, I couldn't find a foothold, and that was as far as I could go. I must have looked like a prairie dog sticking its head out of its den. My only option was to thrust my arms out through the breach and use my upper body to haul myself upwards.

Which I finally did, but at the expense of both of my triceps, which strained, then ripped, then tore themselves to shreds. I rolled around the mountain floor for twenty minutes, eyes closed, tears streaming down my face, screaming in agony. When I finally opened my eyes and looked around, I realized I was five feet from the edge of the cliff.

There was no guardrail of any kind.

But, my closest brushes with death occurred not in any wilderness, but upon the streets of New York City. In the Bronx, a kindly gentlemen forced his way into my car as I got in, holding a knife to my throat. He requested my car keys and my cash. In the interest of forthrightness and complete disclosure, I announced that I possessed forty dollars and that he was certainly welcome to it. I added, however, that I was quite attached to my vehicle, and that if he wanted *that* he would have to kill me.

He considered this carefully for a moment, and I was more than willing to await his decision, which was gratefully in my favor. He settled for the cash.

An early evening stroll down 125th Street in Manhattan resulted in an unexpected conference with a rather vibrant young man who held a .38 caliber revolver to my chest and demanded my wallet. It was broad daylight. I looked at his gun. Then, I looked to my right, then to my left, and asked him to do the same. He was happy to comply, but I'm sure he didn't understand where I was going with all this.

I was pleased to provide an explanation. I advised him that the streets were filled with people, and while I would probably wind up dead soon after this happy affair had concluded, there was also a significant possibility that he would end up in jail for a considerable period of time.

He seemed to consider this carefully, and I was also willing to wait for *his* decision. That it was a difficult one, I understood, really, I did. After all, he was six-foot-two and had a handgun. I was five-foot-five and armed with only a few lines of baloney.

But I wasn't willing to wait *that* long. Growing quite impatient after a time, I demanded that he "put that toy away and go home." A quizzical look flashed across his features and after a moment or so, he holstered his weapon and continued on his way. I sighed and checked my watch, annoyed that I was now late for my engagement.

But my most memorable experience in this regard was one that was *truly* uneventful and noteworthy only because it was. Forgive me that it cannot be related to you in a lighthearted manner.

On the evening of July 30, 1977, I was enjoying a night of partying with my good college buddy, Wayne, who had rented a house in the Bath Beach area of Brooklyn. I was accompanied to this wild affair by a lovely young lady.

At about 2:00 a.m., on the morning of July 31, and somewhat

inebriated, I suggested to my date that we take a moonlight stroll. I remembered I was quite happy and that it was a beautiful evening. We walked through the streets of Brooklyn, hand in hand, returning to the party some time later and leaving soon thereafter.

The next morning I received a call from Wayne that chilled my blood, and that does so once more as I relate this tale.

At about 2:35 a.m., on the morning of July 31, in the Bath Beach area of Brooklyn, just two blocks from Wayne's home, a twenty-year-old woman was brutally murdered and her date critically injured by David Berkowitz, known then as the .44 Caliber Killer, and known forever thereafter as the *Son of Sam*. He had terrorized the city for over a year, murdering young couples in the early hours of the morning. Up to that time, he had committed his carnage exclusively in the boroughs of Queens and the Bronx. There was little reason for police to think he would attempt his crimes anywhere else. It was his first kill in Brooklyn and the last time he murdered anyone.

We were his ideal victims, my girlfriend and I – his *modus operandi* – and there is little reason for me to think that we didn't saunter right by him, or that he didn't observe us with keen and calculated interest as we wandered those dark streets at that early morning hour.

Whew.

OK, I'm through. I really do need to get back on track and return to my original story. Thousands of you are impatiently tapping your fingers on your night tables and I can see some of you rolling your eyes even from here. I probably brought you *down* a little with those last few paragraphs, I know, and I'm sorry, but a part of me needs to be thorough. Besides, it's the bad stuff that makes you need the comedy even more.

Maybe this is a good time to tell you that I did *not* publish this book myself. Somebody actually *allowed* me to write this crazy stuff in this rambling, madcap manner. His name is John Hunt, and he's my publisher, and he's a really great guy. He genuinely seems to *enjoy* it, too. Well, there's no accounting for taste. Hell, maybe *you* like this stuff, too, and perhaps that makes *all* of us a little *berserko,* if you know what I mean.

Yeah; I think that's it.

Back to the Glades.

So there I was, and here you are with me again. I was sixty miles deep into the park, and the road had ended, and civilization had ended, and only the jungle was before me. In a space of two days I had done my level best to drown and transform myself into shark bait; I had tempted a gathering of Nosferatu-like insects with an irresistible treat; and, I had offered myself up as a hot meal to alligators. I was beginning to feel like the fast food of the animal kingdom.

But I wasn't through. You see, once I set out to do something, I really try to get it done.

It's all about personal responsibility.

So, without a moment's thought or hesitation, I selected a path that looked like a trail and proceeded into the dense bush. I concede that it occurred to me as I walked, that the little byway I was rambling upon might not be a trail at all, but little more than a rarely-used pathway for tree frogs, or a mere parting of the foliage caused by the recent travels of a massive carnivore of one kind or another that was not only waiting for me just up ahead, but adjusting its napkin and rearranging its silverware in anticipation of my imminent arrival.

Coincidentally, in seconds, I came to a fork. I turned right. Brazenly, I didn't even employ my signal light. I must have thought I had the right of way.

Moments later, I came to an identical junction and did the same. In just a few steps, I came to a similar intersection. I stopped and looked back in the direction from which I had come. The clearing I had started from had disappeared from view and all I could see was rain forest. OK. This little jaunt was not turning out as I had planned.

Now I am a *Gemini,* and a *true* Gemini in every sense of the word. I proceed on these little ventures complete with pockets teeming with caution and a backpack overflowing with recklessness. There's simply no telling from which I will partake at any given time. But, at least at that moment, it was easy to discern that I could lose my way without much further effort. I elected to exercise a bit more prudence and decided to turn back in a few more yards.

So I traveled on a bit and, unexpectedly, came to another clearing. Not unexpectedly, I found I had company.

There is a certain type of bird found in relative abundance across these United States and it's called a turkey vulture. Let me assure you that a turkey vulture looks *nothing* like a turkey. *Nothing* about it will remind you of that unfortunate guest of honor invited to all of our Thanksgiving dinners.

It looks *exactly* like a vulture; like every single vulture in every single movie in which you've ever seen a vulture. These animals usually feast on carrion, as all vultures do, and have a four-foot wingspan. They will circle the sky or sit on a tree branch or park themselves by the side of a road – and patiently, at that – wait for a dead *something,* or *soon-to-be-dead-something* upon which to dine. Occasionally, they're not willing to wait at all.

They may travel around in solitary fashion or, if they prefer, accompanied by a circle of colleagues and associates. A group of them taking to the air simultaneously will make a sound reminiscent of the galloping hooves of a herd of horses.

Which is what the fifty or so turkey vultures did when I happened onto their nesting site.

And, because I can usually be relied upon to do *something* stupid on most every holiday I take, I thought this was a *wonderful* opportunity to take some pictures, which I proceeded to do, as the birds circled in the air and dive-bombed to the earth, their wings and talons brushing the top of my head as they did.

You're being attacked, the Gremlin offered.

"HAH!" I said to the Gremlin, thinking I had finally caught it using a *four*-word expression instead of a three-word phrase.

You're an idiot, it replied, rudely reminding me that contractions counted as one word.

Also, that *I* was not making any of the rules here and that I had little control over the radio in my brain.

When my feathered friends began to get a bit too close – so close that I could see how *irritated* they really were – I decided to retreat to the relative safety of the jungle.

I managed to take over forty pictures. Not one of them came out. But I *did* get a *really cool feather* as a souvenir.

So, I survived long enough to get back to my hotel room where I was compelled to realize how *dense* I truly am.

When I go on these little expeditions, I always carry two things with me: first, I take my camera and second, I take a knife. I always use the former, I've never required the latter, and I'm not sure why I limit myself to only these two items.

Food, water and a compass might be helpful; I don't know. I've never really given it much thought, which illustrates only that I'm often disinclined to take my *intellect* along.

I guess I prefer to travel light.

Notwithstanding, you may recall that this essay began with a description of an uneventful little journey on a catamaran. That jaunt lasted hours, from beginning to end, all of it taking place in the glorious Florida sunshine. And certainly, there would be little point in a New Yorker spending all of that time on a boat without catching a few rays, as they say.

I'm not referring to that baseball team in Tampa, nor making reference to the sea animal of the same name. I'm talking about a *suntan,* which I intended to come home with just like any other tourist, if for no other reason than to prove that I went *somewhere.* So I lounged shirtless on the deck for hours, coming and going, gathering evidence of my trip.

Obviously, neither a knife nor a camera will protect you against *sunburn*, no matter how many of each you may choose to carry with you, and I didn't carry a knife with me on this occasion anyway. Nor did I see fit to pack along any sunscreen, largely because sunscreen is quite useless as a weapon and can't be employed to preserve any of your fond holiday memories. Thus, it's a totally unnecessary addition for a man the likes of me to carry along.

But by the time I hit the Everglades, I realized I had nearly roasted myself alive on that ship, said roasting having occurred primarily on my back, because I spent most of my nautical sunbathing lying on my stomach. However, being somewhat distracted by the various *animalistic* assaults described here, I was able to hold off the agony, which steadily increased throughout the day, much like the mercury rises in any Floridian's thermometer as the day progresses.

Nor did I have the presence of mind to acquire any insect repellent before my jungle adventure because...well...*you know*.

At the risk of repeating myself – and I am willing to take that risk – I'm a *true Gemini*, possessing both high intellect and simplemindedness in equal proportion. Both are on display when I prepare for any trip. As to the former, I make sure to familiarize myself with all of the local fauna, insects, fish and other animals I may tend to run into on my journeys. In this way, I can determine what is dangerous and what is not, if, by chance, I'm unexpectedly invited to dinner by anything. In this regard, as I've explained, I'm rarely requested as a guest, sometimes intended as an appetizer and usually expected to be the main course.

So, having returned to my hotel room, I became forcefully aware of a pain in the area of my back which was now significantly exceeding that of any mere sunburn. It was more akin to what the gentle warmth of a supernova might produce. I walked into the bathroom, removed my shirt, turned around and looked over my shoulder into a mirror.

Chiggers are a charming species of mite, similar to ticks, and most commonly found in hot and humid regions of the southeastern United States. They're unusual in that they tend to congregate in packs, like wolves, and they're not content to merely *bite* you. Rather, they *digest you* after injecting enzymes into your skin that make you suitable for this purpose. The mark they leave is somewhat distinct to a trained eye, as is the intense itching and swelling which is the typical result of their repast.

Wikipedia casually refers to a human being as a chigger's *accidental* host, as it appears these delightful *bug-a-boos* prefer *animals* as opposed to *manimals*.

While I suppose that even an *insect* can make a little mistake every now and then, in my case, a group of them had screwed up *real bad.* More accurately, an entire dinner party had descended upon the area of my sunburn with all of the accuracy of a laser-guided missile, and partied like it was 1999, although *that* year was still a decade away at the time.

There were thirty-seven of them, to be exact. How could I be sure? Well, I counted the fiery red, swollen, *itchy* wounds on my skin, of course.

That evening was hell on earth, as I writhed in my bed in agony, cursing myself for my lack of forethought and wondering whether this was just God's way of telling me I had been single long enough.

I decided that was the case, so I went back home to New York and proposed to my bride. Whatever fears I had in this regard, whatever trepidation remained, whatever doubts I still had about getting betrothed, one thing was sure:

Marriage had to be a lot *safer* than any Florida vacation.

The Ring

IT IS TRUE, of course, that many people influence us throughout our lives, and perhaps none much more so than our parents. Each have so many roles to fill, you see: that of friend, confidant, protector, disciplinarian, and teacher. We interact with them intimately throughout our lives, seeing them at their very best and at their very worst: in times of sadness and joy, disappointment and exhilaration. Undoubtedly, we form opinions about them. Ultimately, we feel we know them.

Or sometimes, we merely think that we do. Every rare once in a while, we're permitted to glimpse aspects of their true personalities, hidden even from their children. And sometimes these glimpses come in the form of snapshots that pierce the veil of life and death itself, offered not from the living, but from beyond the grave.

Almost a half century ago, my father received a gift from a friend lying on his deathbed. It was a white gold, diamond and sapphire pinky ring that the man had worn his entire life, and he gave it to my father as a symbol of their enduring affection and friendship. For the rest of his life, my father wore that ring on his finger. Over the years it became a part of his persona and his wardrobe, and he never removed it from his hand; until Thanksgiving Day, in 2005, just two months before his death at the age of eighty.

While it would be disingenuous to suggest that I don't enjoy some of the finer things in life (particularly beautiful hotels in the Caribbean and single malt scotches) I've never been the kind of person that looked at life's prime objective as the accumulation of money and personal possessions. As pertained to my father, there was nothing he owned that I desired so much as to compel me to request of him, at any point in his life, "...*when you die, can I have <u>that</u>?*"

I add – only in passing – that my two beautiful daughters have diverged from this philosophy. At least once a year they can be found conferencing with each other, in the most serious of tones, having surrounded themselves with the entirety of my wife's rather expansive (and still expanding) collection of jewels and baubles, which they empty from her two burgeoning jewelry boxes onto our California king-sized bed. There, they negotiate over each piece, divvying the proceeds in advance, so to speak. More accurately, they put in their claims to their favorite pieces *now*, rather than wait for my wife's unfortunate demise, thereby averting the avoidable unpleasantries of fisticuffs over, say, a strand of pearls at the eulogy.

Failing to agree on any one item, they will each petition their dear mother – arguing their points and their perceived rights *to whatever* with great alacrity – oblivious only to the fact that their mother is still sucking in oxygen and probably will be for quite some time yet. Yet, patience is a virtue, I suppose, and I further suppose that their mom should be grateful that they're willing to wait at all.

Be that as it may, my father's ring was my exception to my rule. I considered this piece of jewelry my birthright. I was the eldest son, after all, and it was the only thing he possessed that I wished to carry with me when he died. As the ring was given to him as a token of love and affection, so would I wear it, as a symbol of my father's love, and pass it down to another one day, who would wear it with a similar regard.

I never really considered the issue, never discussed the ring with him at all, and was quite willing to wait until he actually passed – really, I was – when, I assumed, it would enure to me by operation of one law or the other.

I am my father's son, I imagine, for better or worse, but it cannot be said that my brother is. Somewhat differently inclined, and more concerned with certainty and proper planning, he decided that there was little to be gained by waiting until the last minute when it came to such affairs. Put another way, *he* wanted the ring. And he got it, too, but not in quite the manner he might have anticipated.

So, back to Thanksgiving, 2005. Dad wasn't well, and I guess we all knew it; each of us was preparing ourselves in our own small ways, as he was. As upset as I was over his physical condition, we were just not getting along. There was something that needed to be said between us, something that needed to be resolved, and it was left hanging, like fruit left too long on a tree branch to rot.

Before Thanksgiving dinner, Dad made an "announcement," and it was this: He said he'd decided to give me the object of my desire, but now, not in a will or testament. With that, he took the ring off of his finger and presented it to me.

Tears welled in my eyes. It was a touching sentiment, designed to meet an unvoiced wish. I also took the gift as a moving display of affection from my father and I reacted accordingly. Until.

Until my brother and father starting laughing simultaneously. Until.

Until my brother showed me the ring on *his* finger, a duplicate of the one I'd just placed on mine. I was confused, but an explanation was forthcoming.

My father had somehow become aware that both of his sons sought the same piece of jewelry. Matt had asked for it directly; I had not. There was no way of satisfying us both, so, as it was explained to me at the time, Dad decided to give my brother the original ring, as he had expressed his wish for it first, and then commissioned a jeweler to craft its duplicate, which he presented to me. Why he thought it necessary to make a joke out of the affair, or how my momentary belief that I'd been gifted with the original could somehow have caused the pair mirth, eluded me. I wasn't interested in the ring as an *object,* but as a legacy, and as a symbol of my father's love. I had little interest in the copy. It all seemed a cruel joke and it did not make for a pleasant Thanksgiving.

Eight years passed. My father spent seven years and ten months of that time in a plot in New Jersey.

I live my life by a set of rules I've developed over the years. Each of my rules represents a serious mistake I've made. By making these rules, I vow never to repeat the errors they epitomize. One of them is this: never underestimate anyone. It would take eight years for me to realize that this rule encompassed my father, whose wisdom would become apparent long after he had died.

The issue of the ring came up at one of the weekly dinners I enjoy with my now aged mother; how or why I'm not sure. With that dinner came a revelation, as well as an explanation for Dad's actions on that Thanksgiving so long ago.

The Judgment of Solomon is an ancient tale of a ruler's great wisdom, recounted in the Bible, where the famous king was presented with two women, each of whom claimed they were the mother of the same infant son. Solomon decreed that the only fair solution was to take a sword and slice the baby in half, with one half going to each of the women. One resisted the solution, insisting that the baby must live. She released her claims upon it, thereby revealing the child's genuine parent to the great king.

My father had been faced with a similarly intractable dilemma that defied a simple resolution. Both of his sons desired the same object. His youngest son had asked for it first. His eldest had made no such request but expected the ring to be bequeathed to him without him having to. There was no way to please us both, and no way to satisfy the right we both claimed.

Or was there?

It said that dead men tell no tales, but they do; they continue to communicate long after they've died, through the living. It was through my mother that I learned of my father's strangely astute solution.

Dad didn't believe in a *no-win* scenario. In his mind, he avoided one by creating a duplicate of the ring. He gave the *copy* to my brother, allowing him to believe he had received the original. To me, he gave the *original*, convincing *me* that it was the facsimile by adding a bit of theatrics. For eight years, I wallowed in ignorance of his peculiar logic.

As it was explained to me, Dad believed my birthright to be superior to my brother's stated desire. It was enough for him to know that he had granted my wish and that justice had been served, only without offending the more delicate sensibilities of his younger son. I had gained what I so desired, but I was not destined to learn that I had. My sibling was to remain similarly ignorant, although perhaps more satisfied with the result; a solution that might have impressed Solomon himself.

The only question left, then, was whether I should tell my brother the truth. With a wink of my eye and a nod of my head to dear old Dad, I decided to keep his secret a secret.

Until.

Until my brother came into the office one day, terribly distressed, and advised me that he had lost Dad's ring. He had taken it off in a washroom, forgot it there, and lost it.

Except, he hadn't; not really.

So, with a sad smile on my face, I told him the secret our father had taken to his grave. And, at a time when he would be most likely to welcome the tale.

Somewhere, perhaps, Dad was smiling, too.

Max

HIS NAME WAS MAX and he grew up in Brooklyn. He was a former Marine sergeant and served in the Second World War. He was a big guy and a tough son of a bitch and words in the form of hoarse orders spewed from his mouth as easily as his ready laugh, which was always followed by a grin so broad it seemed it could connect California to New York.

And once upon a time, in Brooklyn, New York, Max met a woman, and her name was Adele, and he fell in love with her and married her, and they had children together and stayed together for life. And it was a good life.

Max was a dear friend of my father. Adele was a childhood friend of Mom. I knew them both my entire life. Max always treated me as a son, and I loved him for it.

And one day Max and Adele took the kids and moved to Arizona, and they got old there, and they died there, one soon after the other. And then they came back to Brooklyn together one last time.

I don't know exactly what moves a person to wish to be cremated, but some do. The way Max thought about it, I guess, was that he wished to be buried in Brooklyn, which he still considered his home. But he also knew that his family was now 2000 miles away from that place and couldn't be counted on to visit him there. No one he had known in Brooklyn was alive to come to his gravesite, either. So, he decided to be cremated, and his wife agreed, and they decided that their ashes were to be spread on the beach in Coney Island, where they had spent so many happy times together.

So Max requested that his family and friends visit him one last time, back there in Brooklyn, just off the boardwalk, in the shadow of the Parachute Jump and the Wonder Wheel.
And they did.

And so did I.

We all sat on a picnic table, in front of Nathan's, right by the sea, and everyone ate hot dogs and French fries, and looked at pictures and shared our memories. Then each of us was given a slender plastic tube, and each tube contained ashes, the mortal remains of Adele and Max, in equal proportion, we were told. Together.

We turned and all walked out onto the beach. It was a bright spring day, and the brisk sea air smelled wonderful, and all around us were laughing children and hawking vendors, and people taking pictures, and riding bicycles, and walking dogs, and eating cotton candy. My ears were filled with the screams of kids on the Thunderbolt, and I looked over my shoulder to see the mad-capped mug of the park's famous Alfred E. Newman look-alike over the gate separating the boardwalk from the new Luna Park, all getting smaller and smaller as I walked towards the water's edge.

One of Max's grandkids was there, and she had never been on a beach; she had never seen the ocean.

"I had no idea it would look like this," she said, as she stared in amazement.

I smiled at her innocent remark as I turned and gazed over the water. "This is the Atlantic Ocean," I said. "This is where your grandfather wanted to be."

I thought of Max as I walked, and that smile of his, and that crazy laugh of his, and how he used to slap me on the back every time he saw me. Tears came to my eyes as I thought of the times we had shared, and with those tears came a realization. You might call it a greater appreciation for the scope of the sad duty bestowed upon the members of our stalwart group.

Then I began to ponder something I was already aware of: that the plastic tube I was carrying contained the remains of *two* people, co-mingled, as they were. I don't know why I started to think about this, but I did.

And when I thought about it for a little longer, I realized that I really didn't know *who or what* was in these tubes at all. For a moment, I started to feel really *eeekkked* out, if you know what I mean.

"OK, slow down," I mumbled to myself. I had to come to grips with the fact that small remnants of my friends were in these vials, in what proportion I could only guess.

But which parts? I mean, was I holding the remains of Adele's big toe and Max's testicles?

Then I remembered that Max had only *one* testicle. Something had happened to the other one – I really don't remember what – but as I recall the other functioned quite well on its own, thank you very much. For some strange reason, I choked out a gravelly chuckle. I wondered whether Max was laughing right at this moment, wherever he was.

I wondered a bit less when another thought occurred to me.

The beach was crowded.

No.

The beach was *extraordinarily* crowded. People were sunbathing, having full meals on blankets, drinking under umbrellas and reading books as they lay on the sand. Kids were running back and forth with beach balls and footballs and soccer balls; throwing Frisbees to each other, and trying to persuade the wind to catch their kites.

Did I mention it was a windy day?

It was a *very* windy day.

Ten people were going to spread the ashes of my two beloved friends onto the sand of an extraordinarily crowded beach on a very windy day.

An image of Max holding his stomach in laughter flashed across my mind.

I stopped and turned around. I had walked perhaps thirty yards, and it was about one hundred more yards to the water. I noted that the wind was coming from the direction of the ocean and that the crowd was a bit thinner where I was standing. I could actually see a clear path to the boardwalk every now and then, with no people zigzagging back and forth.

In short, I thought maybe we could pull this off right there, without any part of Max being picked up by an errant breeze, only to become part of someone's turkey sandwich.

Then I noticed that not all of our party had advanced upon the beach as far as I had. One of the more elderly participants was arguing with one of Max's kids, advising that she was unable to make the long walk to the ocean, as the offspring was apparently suggesting. The woman – an octogenarian, it appeared – was summarily deserted to remain on the boardwalk to await the troupe's return. I couldn't tell if her assignment of ashes were confiscated from her as a further penalty for her sorry lack of cooperation and her dismal failure to appreciate the *spirit* of the occasion.

I waited for the entire group to catch up with me. The husband of one of Max's daughters came to my side. He was burdened with an array of cameras, tripods and other electronic devices slung over his shoulders. For some reason, he reminded me of a wartime correspondent.

He suggested to the group that we all form a circle, say a few words and scatter the ashes we were holding. I crooked my finger at him, beckoning him closer, suggesting he humor me with a brief conference.

"I recommend that you keep your back to the wind," I whispered into his ear.

He looked at me – momentarily bewildered – until a particularly strong gust clarified the meaning of my proposal.

"I see," was his only reply, as he wisely turned his back to the ocean, and the wind, and abandoned his notion of forming a mystical ring, which I'm sure might have assisted our dearly departed cross over, as it were, but which would've also assured that half our party would've been dusted with their remains. He was now prepared to complete the task at hand.

His wife would have none of this. She declared that she was wading into the ocean and depositing her share of ashes there. The implication of her remark was that we should all do the same. I realized that to follow her example would be to convert the entire affair into something more akin to a baptism than a funeral. I also realized I was wearing $200 shoes. Then another thought occurred to me.

Was any of this *legal*? Surely this had to be against the law. You can't just toss the remains of dead people anywhere you choose.

Can you?

Another image of Max crossed my mind. This time he was rolling around on the floor in hysterics, curled into a fetal position, begging me to stop.

As we advanced towards the water the beach-going throngs seemed to multiply, the crowds becoming thicker and thicker. Our party began to disperse.

Max's daughter waded into the water. Her two teenage daughters – Max's grandkids – walked hand in hand down the beach, scattering their share of ashes as they did. It was touching and quite beautiful, and the sight of them tenderly dispersing the remains of their grandparents along the shoreline made for a memorable snapshot in its way.

It was marred only by the sight of their father back-stepping down the beach in advance of his daughters. He was in his full cinematic glory – acting as cameraman, director and producer of his own *Greatest Moments* motion picture – armed with a digital single-lens reflex camera in one hand, a camcorder in the other, and a light meter strung around his neck, all of which he operated as he barked commands to his offspring, including this precious directorial snippet:

"Girls, you've got to give me more."

Four of our party decided to form a circle after all. For some reason, I just let them do it, without protest of any kind. I guess I was kind of overwhelmed.

They said a few kind words and scattered the contents of their tubes upon the sand. They were oblivious to the fact that the already high gusts were significantly more *gustful* at the water's edge where they were standing.

The result was predictable. In the next moment the remains of Adele and Max – or a few tubes worth of them, anyway – were carried away by the prevailing winds and deposited back in the direction from which they had been released, specifically, onto a female participant's bright green slacks. She giggled like a schoolgirl, apparently out of embarrassment.

Oops!

I thought about Max's testicle again.

The woman brushed Max and Adele off of her pants. I gasped. I tried to compose myself.

About twenty feet from the shore I turned to face the boardwalk and dropped to my knees. I opened the cap on my small tube. I let the sounds of the wind and the crowds fill my ears. The majestic Cyclone rose before my eyes, and with it came ghostly memories of fortune tellers and freak shows and games of chance and of Steeplechase Park. I thought of old photos, and old movies, and tried to remember what Coney Island must have looked like in the 1950s.

I thought of Adele and Max going on countless dates here, walking hand-in-hand along the shoreline, much like their grandchildren had done today.

My friends had returned to their home, to their happy place, where their love for each other first began to bloom.

Maybe this wasn't such a bad place to wind up after all, I thought to myself.

Thomas Wolfe wrote that you can't go back home to your childhood, or to romantic love, or to the old forms of things which once seemed everlasting. You can't go back home to the escapes of Time and Memory, he wrote.

But perhaps he was wrong. Perhaps some people form an eternal connection with the places they consider their homes, one that remains unbroken no matter how far they may stray from them. Perhaps we only get to have one real home in our lives, and that some of us will feel a need to return to it, at one point or another, in this life, or in the next.

With a sad tear in my eye, I slowly spread their ashes across the sand.

I said my goodbyes, and I left.

As I did, a breeze picked up and my shirt buffeted around me.

I could swear I felt a slap on my back.

Scared *Straight*

THE CALL CAME IN AT 10:30 AT NIGHT and I was half-asleep.

It was my vice president and he was a great guy. Meaning not only that was he extremely competent at what he did, but that he was a really great boss and that he liked me.

So, he called me and I was half-asleep. And he started screaming right away. He had never screamed at me before. Hell, he'd never raised his voice to me. I couldn't understand what he was saying, because nothing he was saying made any sense. Even if he *had* been making sense, I was only hearing half of what he was saying, that half being heard by the half of my brain that was awake. It was only clear that he was very, very angry.

He yelled for a few minutes. He told me to be in his office in Manhattan at six the following morning. He hung up: so abruptly, so violently, that it seemed as if a medium-range nuclear missile had detonated somewhere in my inner ear.

Now, I was *wide* awake. I sat up in bed – bug-eyed – as if my eyelids were being held open by a combination of Crazy Glue and some kind of industrial staple used to secure wings to the body of an airplane.

I was running a private trade school at the time, owned by the largest company of its kind in America. I was good at my job and everyone seemed to agree that I was. Yeah, it was *something* like being a *principal,* except that it wasn't.

You see, there are two main differences between a *public* school and a *private* school. First, there is a profit motive in a private school. The director of such a school is expected to *earn money,* just like anyone running any kind of business is expected to. Second, while both institutions are highly regulated, the administrator of a private school is free to do all manner of things that a public school principal cannot. He's given leeway and an outlet for his creativity; he can be more innovative and he has more control over his school.

In short, if he has the ability and the leadership skills, he's given the opportunity to create a model institution. He's permitted to make people *happy* as well – students, parents, faculty and staff – and create the kind of family atmosphere that only the best of companies enjoy and that only the very best administrators are able to create.

I've always believed that the happiness of these four groups of people is the high water mark for a school director. It's proof that he's succeeded at his job. I also believe that if you can help people achieve this state, money will flow naturally as a result. And, if it does, a private school director may find that he can do just about *anything* with his business that he wishes.

Well, not *quite anything*. But that's the story.

Back to Tom, my vice president. He was, and is today, a tall and strikingly handsome man. He was also a lawyer, and a Southerner, carrying with him a North Carolina drawl compelling enough to charm a bee out of its honey. He had a business philosophy that was ideal for a guy like me, and it was this: as long as you bring in the cash, you can do whatever you want.

Now don't think for a second that Tom wasn't concerned about the quality of the schools his directors were running because he was. That's why he took such care when he hired them and made sure they had all the resources they required to do their jobs. But once they had proven themselves as competent, he basically just sat back, let them run their schools as they saw fit, and waited on the sidelines to see if there was anything he could do to assist them.

However, the warm and cuddly and charming Tom I had known was noticeably absent when he made that call. And, even though I was now fully alert, I was still unable to determine what he was so furious about.

It was now 11 o'clock at night and I still had seven hours before the time he had commanded me to appear in his Manhattan office. I had plenty of time to think and I used that time wisely.

Namely, to panic. And, to consider all the things I might've done wrong.

"Stop panicking," I said to myself. "Everyone loves you. You run a great school, you comply with the law and you bring in the dough. The parents are happy, the students are happy, the staff and faculty are happy; everyone's happy. You're the golden boy. You're the main man, the big cheese, the hot tamale. This is just a silly misunderstanding."

And then...I had a thought.

"Well, there was that *one* time when..."

Then, I had another thought.

"Well, yes, there was also that *isolated* incident where..."

I had a third thought.

"Well, and yes, there was that *small* matter of the..."

Uhhhhh, I had done a *lot* of things wrong. It was just that no one had *found out* about them.

Had they?

Now literally gasping for breath, I picked up the phone and with a trembling hand called another company VP with whom I enjoyed an excellent relationship. He was highly disciplined, incredibly intelligent and a superb administrator.

He was also a biblical scholar and, therefore, a reasonable substitute for a priest, which was what I *really* required, because I intended to make a confession. Actually, quite a few of them.

And I did. I told my superior all the things I'd done wrong during my tenure with the company. I asked if any of these might be grounds for termination.

He replied in a kind, soft-spoken and nurturing manner. He assured me that everything I told him would be kept in the strictest confidence. He told me how much affection he had for me, and what a great job I was doing for the company. He said he would stand behind me 100 percent.

Oh, and yes: I *could* be fired for those little episodes. Actually, for any *one* of them.

The Gremlin spoke to me as I hung up the phone.

You are <u>doomed</u>, the Gremlin said.

For some reason, three *phrases* entered my head right after the Gremlin spoke its three words: unemployment insurance, food stamps and bankruptcy proceedings.

Dead, Dead, Dead, my Gremlin reiterated.

I showed up at Tom's office at seven the next morning. I didn't arrive at six as he had instructed, only because the school in which his office was located didn't open until seven. I assumed he did not wish me to loiter outside on the street for an hour, waiting for the front doors to be unlocked.

Of course, that was only an assumption.

I was escorted into a common waiting area usually reserved for prospective students, copy machine repairmen, textbook salesmen and people awaiting job interviews. I fully believed I would soon fall into that latter category of individuals.

Two hours later, Tom popped his head into the waiting room. He glanced at me strangely, then beckoned to a well-dressed man who in all probability was my replacement. The young gentleman – equipped with perfect bridgework, a healthy tan and an immaculate Brooks Brothers suit – accompanied Tom out of the room with a glorious smile upon his face.

Dead and buried, said the Gremlin.

I told the Gremlin to shut the hell up. Everyone in the room looked at me and glared. I realized I had spoken the words out loud. I let my head slump into my hands.

By 11 o'clock a secretary entered and announced, "Tom will see you, now." She turned and exited rapidly, obviously a demure and sensitive thing and way too delicate to stomach a bloody summary execution or gruesome public hanging. I walked alone down a dim hallway leading to Tom's office. If ever there was a last mile, this was surely it.

I knocked on Tom's door. There was no response. I knocked

again; a little harder this time. Nothing. Taking a deep breath, I turned the knob slowly, closed my eyes tightly and opened the door. As I did, please understand that in every single way I felt like that guy you've seen in a thousand movies who is compelled to choose between cutting the blue wire or the green wire on an explosive device.

Tom was sitting at full attention behind his immaculate, broad, cherry wood desk. He looked like a judge about to offer a prisoner a choice of three sentences: death by firing squad, death by lethal injection, or death by a thousand cuts.

Or put another way, *death*.

I told you! the Gremlin screamed.

This time I ignored the little bastard.

I sat down in an oversized armchair, which made me feel considerably smaller than my 5-foot-5-inch frame. I held my knees with both hands to keep them from knocking together. The only thing that caused me any pause was the fact that Tom still had this strange, puzzled look on his face.

He spoke, his southern inflection on full display.

"Dayyyyve," he said, dispensing with any requisite formality or greeting and obviously electing not to dilly-dally, "I got a distuuurbing call yestuhday..."

Despite my considerable trepidation I was mildly intrigued. He continued, not mincing any words.

"...I got a call from a person yesterday who said three things about you..."

That's a coincidence, the Gremlin replied in my brain, demonstrating that it never loses its sense of humor, even in the direst of situations.

Tom paused and I took the opportunity to adjust my collar. After all, while my suit may have been a Sears Roebuck special, my shirt was an *Armani*, and I certainly didn't want *that* to be ruined by any random blood splatter when the ax fell.

I waited for him to offer the punch line. Which, as it turned out, was exactly what he delivered.

"The caller said this," Tom said, "*First,* that you are *gay. Second,* that you are having *sec-tu-al re-lay-tions* with your male staff members. And *third,* that you are having sex with men on yowr *desk* at 3 p.m. each day whiiiile yowr staff listens outside yowr *dooowr.*"

I looked at him blankly, my mouth dropped open, my tongue lolled about like that of a thirsty poodle after a marathon.

""Dayyyyve..." he pleaded, distress and bewilderment plainly written all over his face, *"Are you gaaayyy?"*

While I've previously pointed out to you that nearly every story you'll read here ends in a gay and happy fashion, it occurs to me now that readers should be cautioned against interpreting that phrase too *literally.*

I responded in the *only* way any red-blooded, heterosexual American male possibly could; I laughed hysterically, and I did so for about a minute, holding my stomach with two hands, tears pouring copiously from my eyes. I eventually composed myself, wiping the water from my eyelids with my forearms. Tom looked on, still terribly confused, but with a look of keen embarrassment slowly creeping across his features.

"Toooom," I replied – reflexively and unintentionally mimicking his southern drawl – "the *only* thang *funny* about *me* is mahhh *sense-a-humor!*"

I concede my remark was in terrible taste, but I *was* rather relieved that only my *gayness* was at issue here.

I add – and again, only for the record – that one of my only admirable qualities is that I'm not a judgmental kind of guy. In fact, one of the ancillary themes of this little book is how dangerous it can be to judge or pre-judge people, or place them into tidy little categories based on slim evidence, or form broad generalizations about them based upon poorly conceived beliefs, as we humans are so often wont to do.

For myself, I care little if a person is tall or fat, black or white, rich or poor, gay or straight, or anything in-between. I don't even care if your name is *Caitlyn*.

But, that being said, I am perfectly aware of my personal preferences and inclinations. As well, I have an intimate understanding of how *my* private body parts were intended to function *for me*. And the thought of them operating in any other manner... well...is enough to *scare* me.

Enough to scare me *straight*, in a manner of speaking.

To Sleep, Perchance to *SCREAM*

IN *SNAPSHOTS* I ATTEMPTED TO ENTERTAIN YOU with a story called *Asleep at the Wheel,* a group of short vignettes about people who didn't merely *sleep,* but who entered into Rumplestiltskin-like slumbers, worthy of the mad dwarf himself.

Apparently, some of you believed that the trance-like comas I described had *enormous* comedic appeal, notwithstanding that on at least one such occasion one of my friend's sleeping habits almost cost me my life. Knowing this, it took no great leap of logic for me to conclude that you might find it *positively hysterical* to hear how my daughter's *failure* to sleep almost led not only to my death, but to hers, as well.

Not to be crass, but some folks might call you mildly maladjusted.

Not to worry; I call you my loyal readership.

At the age of thirty-eight I decided to remake myself and go to law school. Ultimately, it turned out to be an excellent career path for me. I'm fond of saying that being a litigator in New York City is the only profession where one can profit – and quite substantially – from talking too much, listening too little and acting like an egotistical, arrogant, know-it-all most of the time. There is a charming colloquial expression commonly employed to describe such people. They're called *assholes.* As you may have guessed, my qualifications in this regard are absolutely superb, as many of my colleagues will attest, and do, and with some regularity before the bar.

So, it was a great idea to become a lawyer, but my timing was less than perfect. I had an infant daughter by the time I decided to attempt law school and added a newborn by my third day of school. Perhaps I should have become a doctor instead, because it was a prescription for disaster, and one that I'd written for myself quite expertly, without the need for any medical training at all.

My first daughter had been a dream, sleep-wise, dozing through the entire night by the time she was three months old. But Ariana, my final attempt at fatherhood, was another story. As most parents figure out by the time they have their second child – assuming, of course, that they have survived their opening act – one sleeps and the other doesn't. I don't know why this is so, but it just seems to be the case, and maybe some of you will tell me whether your experiences are on par with mine.

The best thing I can say about Ariana and her sleeping habits is that she was consistent. My Monday through Thursday evenings went something like this: I would walk in the house around 11 p.m., worn out from four hours of mind-bending instruction, only to see my wife passed out on the bed and my eldest daughter, Stephanie, awake and lying beside her watching television. She was young enough not to care how late she was up, and adorable enough to be happy to see her Daddy at most any hour. She would wave gaily to me – a magnificent greeting for a man who believed he would be dead from stress and exhaustion at any moment – and then fall asleep with little prompting soon thereafter.

Ariana would already be asleep at that hour, but this was just a ruse. Years later, of course, she would grow up to be a genius, and despite her sweet and kind nature, she would also grow up to be a *calculating and manipulative genius*, brilliantly kneading and molding the hearts and minds of the adult population around her with her cute little smile, her charming ways, and her mock receptiveness to anything any adult might suggest.

After which, of course, she would do exactly as she wished, a convention she continues to practice to present day and one she carries out with both enthusiasm and adroitness.

Excuse me for a moment.

Sweetheart, I'm writing a book here, and I'm trying to be amusing. Please don't take anything too literally and understand that your daddy is drinking as he writes this. In fact, he's on his third quart of Scotch right now – and it's only 10:00 a.m. – so understand that I really can't take much responsibility for what you're reading. Furthermore – and as I've advised you several times – I expect the money that I've saved for your education to be exhausted by your second year of law school, and this little book can go a long way toward remediating that minor deficiency. So, if I were you, I'd just sit back on that beach in Santa Monica – where you've spent the last three years getting straight A's without the happily avoidable inconvenience of having to attend your classes – and suck it up.

Sorry.

Anyway, as I've said, Ariana would be fast asleep by the time I came home, but I had little doubt that she *knew* I was there. In fact, I could practically *hear* her chuckling – in little infant chortles – thinking about what she had in store for me in a couple of hours.

Actually, in *exactly* a couple of hours. Because at *precisely* 1:00 a.m. the curtain would rise in the Magic Theatre that was my home, and her performance would commence. It started in much the same way, in that wee hour of the morning, with a blood curdling, high-pitched wail that would pierce my soul like a spearhead, spike my eyes open as if both my feet had been thrust into a pot of boiling infant formula, and undoubtedly lead my neighbors to believe that I was some type of anal-retentive Ted Bundy, whose routine and custom required that I initiate my murder and mayhem at a definite and prescribed hour.

In those days – and they were hard days, to be sure – my wife was the provider and I was the house husband. Andrea was killing herself running home health agencies for sixty hours a week, and I was shopping, cleaning, changing diapers and otherwise raising my two children while operating a small consulting business out of my home and going to school at night. Money was always a problem, too, and to say that I was *stressed to the max* is an understatement that any new parent (or any New York Jets fan) fully understands. Notwithstanding, my wife was the breadwinner in those days and she had to wake up and go to work the next day. So, by an unusually rapid and terribly efficient process of elimination, I was the one elected to attend to any little demon residing in my household who thought that Daddy had *certainly* gotten enough shut-eye for one night.

Now, it should come as no surprise to any parent that infants awake in the middle of the night, and that they do so for some period of time after they are born. Most of us are able to take this in stride: at least in *theory*. After all, they're kind of *new* to all of this *life* stuff, and their individual time zones rest somewhere between the Twilight Zone and the Outer Limits. Furthermore, they get hungry at all hours, and they need to be changed when they need to be changed, and none of us really have any choice in the matter. We all get up with a smile on our face, coo at them gently, and attend to their needs with love and enthusiasm.

Don't we?

Not. Particularly when seventeen of the last nineteen and one-half hours of any given day have consisted of unrelenting, grueling physical and mental activity and only one and one-half hours of sleep.

Worse – in fact, *much* worse – was the fact that Ariana never needed to be changed or fed, as neither of these deeds – accomplished routinely by me for the first six months of her life – seemed to delimit or otherwise reduce the decibel level of her truly incredible shrieks, screams and howls, which seemed to convert her into some kind of alien species or native pterodactyl that hadn't been seen on the planet for several millenniums, at least.

It took me longer than it should have to realize that neither hunger nor an innate sense of personal hygiene was motivating the child.

I've forgotten to mention that there's something else that may compel a baby to wake up in the middle of the night: they simply may not feel well. This may result from some kind of gastrointestinal *something or other* which affects them, one of which ailments is commonly referred to as colic.

I was afflicted by colic for the first seven months of my life. This is unusual, as a diagnosis of colic is usually dependent on what doctors call the *rule of threes*; it appears at three weeks of age; it is characterized by three hours of sustained crying, and it disappears at the age of three months. For me, however, this rule was broken most every day, and I'm happy to note that rule breaking became the norm in my adult life, as well.

More to the point, I cried incessantly for *seven* months – and at all hours of the day and night – until I drove my mother quite mad. She tells me that I continue to do so to present day.

Now I've been blessed with one of the most patient and loving mothers on this planet, so it's hard to imagine a force that would compel my life-giver to wish to exterminate me, but at least at one point in time, she did.

This is actually one of my *mother's* snapshots. I know I'm stretching the rules a bit but have a little patience, will ya?

Sheesh. You guys can be really *strict*.

Anyway, all I'm trying to say is that at the age of seven months, when I was still crying for about seven hours a day, creating a new rule of seven, as it were, my mom just *snapped*. She picked up the phone, called my father at work, and announced – quite unceremoniously – that she was going to throw me out of the window.

Did I mention that she was patient and loving? Well, I can prove that she was patient, at least, because she waited for my father to come home before tossing out the baby without regard for the bathwater, so to speak. He was in Long Island – perhaps 25 miles away – and I'm told he arrived home in less than fifteen minutes, demonstrating that it's essential to have at least one parent who doesn't want you dead.

Back to Ariana. Compelled to awake at one o'clock each morning by a tiny alarm clock buried deep in her spleen or somewhere there around; attuned to a circadian rhythm set by Satan himself, she didn't want to be fed, or changed, and I can attest that she wasn't ill in any way.

No: All she wanted was to be held, and in a very specific way, at that. She would stop her screaming only when hoisted high on my shoulder like a sack of potatoes or a bag of concrete. Then I was required to walk around the house as I held her. So I would march around in circles, traveling from my living room to my dining room, to my kitchen and back to my living room. I was not permitted to stop, nor was I allowed to put her down for a moment, or else this diminutive terrorist would recommence the oral waterboarding of her beloved father. I'd repeat this trek, over and over, until 3:30 a.m., when she'd finally fall asleep.

Truth be told, there came a day when *I* wanted to throw her out of the window, a notion I fully credit to dear old Mom who, as I've explained, came up with the idea first. Of course, I cared little for *originality* at the time, and the *only* reason I didn't throw her out of the window was because this would have accomplished absolutely nothing.

We lived in a ranch house. There was no second floor.

In any event, *that* day came. I was smack-dab in the middle of my nightly hike to nowhere. It was 2:45 a.m. And that was when I dared to take Ariana off my shoulder, only for a moment, mind you. That was my crime and the penalty was severe. Unlike any modern code of justice, there was to be only one punishment and it was death by screaming. My infant daughter was judge, jury and executioner and the sentence was carried out immediately. She began to wail the instant I *de-shouldered* her. I held her at arm's length, amazed that anything so small could make a sound *that* friggin' earth-shattering.

I was also amazed by how *unreasonable* she was.

That being said, I had to throw her *somewhere*. So I simply held her at a height of three feet above a couch and dropped her.

It was a symbolic gesture, I know, but sometimes that's all a father has, *you dig?*

I returned to my bedroom and awoke my wife. There were no rules, now. All the usual standards of conduct were abandoned. I announced she was taking care of the child. She got up, I replaced her in the bed, and in moments I was asleep.

Three hours later the screaming began again. I lurched awake, as I usually did, as if a cattle prod had been forced down my throat.

Or if you prefer, thrust *up* somewhere else.

Please note that I didn't *say* what you're obviously *thinking*.

Anyway, I don't know which of my charming offspring initiated the cacophony, and I thought for a moment that it was both of them simultaneously. For a second I considered whether they had stayed up all night, plotting their plot and planning their plan, giggling to themselves as they did, charting with exact precision and perfect timing the most efficient and brutal way of murdering their loving father.

Or maybe in an infantile act of compassion, they had finally decided to put me out of my misery. I didn't know what they may have wanted; I didn't know what their motivation was. I didn't know why an otherwise kind and benevolent Creator would see fit to construct a world where small children wake up bawling, howling and sniveling instead of gurgling cute little baby gurgles and charming the hell out of their parents each and every morning. It really didn't matter anymore.

I took one step from my bed and towards the bedroom my children shared and stopped cold. My wife, who was preparing herself to go to work, stepped into the bedroom at that moment and looked at me quizzically. To her, this was just another day.

I looked back at her in horror and disbelief. I looked at my bed longingly. I glanced in the direction of my children's bedroom, then back at my bed again, and then back in the direction of their bedroom. The sounds coming from that room were incredible, a syncopated symphony of terror that could only have been composed by demons in a comic book world gone insane. I thought I saw the walls vibrating. For some reason, I looked at both of my hands. I could swear I saw them melting, then realized I was hallucinating from lack of sleep.

So I did the only thing I could think of: the only thing a person in my position could do: I took the only logical course of action any thinking, rational, reasonable man could follow.

I threw myself on my bed and cried hysterically, just like they were doing.

My wife sighed and left to take care of the kids. I suppose it was clear to her by that time that I was quite useless as a father, and that she'd basically gotten out of me all that there was to get. I expected to be replaced immediately, and perhaps sent to the same glue factory they used to send horses to when they outlived their usefulness.

When my wife returned to our bedroom – and only, I am sure, to determine whether she needed to summon an ambulance or a mortician – I had composed myself slightly. I rose from the bed and straightened my back. I fixed my hair with my two hands as best I could and straightened the tie I wasn't wearing, still somewhat delirious. I made an announcement, and it was this; these were my words:

"If Ariana doesn't sleep through the night *tonight*, I will *kill* her."

And I meant it, too, God help me, I meant it. My wife smiled at me, a cute little smirk she was inclined to display whenever I announced that I wanted to kill something or someone which, in those days, I did more frequently than I would care to admit. When she looked at me this way, she seemed to be making a statement to me, and posing a question to herself, both at the same time.

The statement was, *"Don't be stupid."* The question was, *"He's going to do it, isn't he?"*

I was dazed and crazed the entire day. I went through the motions of housekeeping and child rearing detached and unemotional. I was more zombie than father, more robot than man, walking around the house with my eyes glazed and my mouth open, shuffling my feet, drooling frequently and not caring that I was.

My two daughters – Chaos and Mayhem – cried intermittently throughout the day, and I was completely unmoved by their tears and wails. The reason was simple. *Somebody* was going to die tonight and all of this was going to be over, one way or the other.

That evening, as I prepared for bed, I commenced a ritual undoubtedly foreign to anyone who is not a Samurai warrior, a Spartan, a professional cage fighter or a gang member.

I took a baseball bat and leaned it against my dresser. On the top of my dresser I placed a long, sharp kitchen knife. Next to the knife, I placed a necktie that I'd fashioned into a noose. Next to the necktie, I positioned a hammer. I took a step back from the dresser and admired my handiwork, considered whether I had properly prepared and determined that I had. If I needed anything else, I could certainly add it to my collection later on.

I turned from the dresser – quite satisfied – and faced my wife, who was sitting up in bed with that demure, adorable, *friggin' idiotic* smile upon her face.

"You thought I was kidding, didn't you?" I asked her.

She had nothing to say. To be fair, I guess *that* type of declaration was hard to follow with a snappy comeback.

I lay down in bed with an enormous smile upon my face, my hands crossed over my chest as if I were a corpse in a box ready for the grave. I breathed deeply and sighed, content for the first time in months.

I guess you always feel better when you're finally able to make a difficult decision.

I closed my eyes and fell asleep.

Some time later, I opened my eyes to sunlight. I heard birds happily chirping away in my backyard.

My wife was gone. The house was silent. The clock on my night table told me it was 9 a.m.

I sat up in bed abruptly, held my breath, and listened.

I wasn't listening for my children. I was listening for sirens.

I looked around my bedroom with some urgency.

I wasn't looking for my kids. I was looking for bloodstains.

I wondered whether I had killed both of them in their sleep.

You might have, the Gremlin said.

"Thanks for the vote of confidence," I replied to myself.

Then, I chuckled, realizing how silly that sounded.

I couldn't have killed them in their sleep. They *didn't* sleep. I could only have murdered them while they were *awake*.

That's a relief, the Gremlin replied.

I rose from my bed, traversed the threshold of my bedroom and turned right. My children's bedroom was only a few yards away. I ambled in slow motion in that direction, my eyes darting back and forth, scanning for bullet holes, blood splatter, body parts, or any other of the delightful indicators of mass murder.

The door to their bedroom was ajar by six inches. I placed a sweaty hand on the doorknob and opened the door. And I saw.

Stephanie was in her little bed snoring a little baby snore. As I approached, she slowly opened her eyes.

"Hi, Da-Da," she said, with a glorious smile upon her face.

"Good morning, sweetheart," I replied.

Slowly I turned – to coin a phrase – and step by step, inch by inch, I approached Ariana's crib.

She was awakening as I did, stretching all four limbs – as cute as she could possibly be – slowly opening her eyes to gaze at her loving father.

"Ihh laaa plah puhhssss," she babbled with an enchanting grin brightening her countenance.

"Hello, baby," I replied as I stroked her hair, tears of relief welling in my eyes.

I turned to leave, took a few steps, stopped, and returned to Ariana's side. She was still smiling, clearly delighted to see me again so soon. I leaned down.

"You've saved your own life," I whispered in her ear.

She frowned.

"Plahh puhh plahh pbbbbb!" she replied, spitting in my face as she did.

Unintentionally, I am sure.

After the First Breath...

MY FIRST CHILD DIDN'T TAKE A BREATH until about two minutes after she was born. My wife was mostly unconscious, and I watched on in horror as two doctors worked on my newborn, trying to encourage her first mouthful of oxygen.

They were professionals; they had done this a thousand times before. Each time a new life had been placed in their hands. Each time, the fate of an entire family – each of them, and all of them together – rested there, as well. They knew the stakes. Sometimes – unbeknownst to anyone else – they knew the odds.

As they labored, subtle, barely observable changes occurred in the features of the two physicians. With each second that passed, their actions became more desperate, and they looked less like highly skilled practitioners and more like mere humans, frantically fighting to preserve an infant's life.

But Stephanie lived to take her first breath, and I survived to watch as her entire body turned from a pale blue to a flesh colored pink, from her head to her toes, as if a wave had fallen over her. She was whisked away by the relieved doctors as I attended to my wife.

A few minutes later our obstetrician returned. He had the broadest smile on his face that I'd ever seen. He was clearly delighted by *something*.

"You have the most beautiful baby in the world!" he exclaimed. You *have* to come and see this child!"

My wife was in good hands, and although I was hesitant to leave her at that moment, a greater temptation to do so I couldn't have imagined.

I left the operating room, turned the corner, and was greeted by an empty hallway. My wife's room was at the far end of it: for some reason that was where I believed my baby had been taken. With a determined stride, I headed in that direction.

I walked by the nursery to my left. In it were a dozen wailing infants, and despite two sets of doors, and the thick safety glass through which you could view the babies, their muffled cries reached my ears. But as I passed that room I froze. I had heard something, something *familiar,* something that riveted me and stopped me cold. So I turned and entered.

I was there for only a moment when my eyes attached to her. It wasn't that I recognized her, or that I could say I had somehow seen her before: in a dream, perhaps, or in another life.

I couldn't say I observed familiar features in her face – a nose, an eyebrow, or a wrinkle – passed down through the ages from one relation or another.

It was her *cry* that I had distinguished, and instantly, and from that of every other child. Even from outside that room, it was the sound of her voice that I could identify, as if I'd been encoded with it from the moment she was born.

I approached her crib.

"Hello, Boo-Boo," I said, tears in my eyes.

These were the words I had whispered to my wife's belly so many times, cooing to my unborn child as the months passed, as Stephanie slowly blossomed in the womb.

As I uttered those words, my baby stopped crying, caught in mid-wail as if suddenly enchanted by the spell of a wizard. She turned her head in my direction and opened her eyes to look at her father for the first time.

We love our children with all of the resolve and might our minds and our bodies possess. We adore them from the instant they are born, from the very first time we see them, from the moment they take their first breath.

We share a bond with them and we know that we do. We are moored to them, like a ship to a dock, by the simple fact of our parentage. We are tethered to them forever by ties fashioned from our tenderness and secured by our devotion. But there is another link between a father and his daughter that is forged in some other way, one that's intangible and obscure, and that is hammered and wrought before they are thrust into this world.

Maybe we are only animals, you and I, no different from the wildebeest that can recognize her calf's call among a hundred others in a herd. Maybe it is that unborn children hear us when we speak to them in the womb. Perhaps they are listening all the while, and that they manage to understand us, somehow, in some way. Maybe they only comprehend that our words are meant for them.

But I have come to believe that the real connection between a father and his daughter is to be found somewhere else, not from a place where the heart resides, but from where the spirit dwells. Perhaps you feel this too.

But this is only evidence that we've given our babies our souls as well as our hearts.

Scrooged!

I WOULD LIKE TO BELIEVE, as we all would, that most people are good people with the best of intentions. We all make mistakes, of course; we all get angry, we all argue and have disagreements and say and do things to each other that we come to regret later on. We all have our bad days and good days, and each and every one of us has woken up in a foul mood once in a while. The point is, the majority of us don't go around trying to *harm* people.

But sometimes – every rare once in a while – we come across people who are just mean-spirited. For whatever reason, these charming folks seem to be at war with the world and everyone in it. To them, *every* day is a bad day and the sole reason they seem to be here is to make everyone around them as miserable as they are.

There's a word for these people. They are called *bastards.*

Or, as we say in *New York*, they're *baahstids.*

Further, sometimes we find an entire *family* of them, all in one place and all at the same time. And, if there is a higher power in this universe, if there is any balance to be found in the cosmos, if there's a natural order to things, even the biggest bunch of *Scrooges* will find themselves *Scrooged* every now and again.

As I've told you and as I'll remind you once again, in my former life I used to be a private school administrator. Specifically, I ran private trade and business schools that taught their students specific vocational skills: anything from watch repair to medical office administration.

One of the unique characteristics of such schools is that sometimes their students actually *learn stuff* and get a *real job* as a direct result of their training.

Amazing, right? It really is a novel concept in the field of education these days.

Of course, the people who own such schools occasionally go

to federal prison for misappropriating student loan funds.

Anyway, there was this school in Manhattan that I worked at once upon a time. It was owned and operated by a man and his wife and his son, all of whom worked there, as well. There was a daughter, too, but she was a drug addict and didn't work at all. But she was sweet, and friendly, and stopped by once in a while just to say hello. And to snort cocaine in the bathroom.

That was the extent of her participation in the enterprise.

I wasn't permitted the luxury of an office. I worked in a *room* with a desk. Across from my desk there was another, and in a chair behind that desk resided the wife, a blonde-haired, middle-aged bimbo who would stare at me all day long as she labored, day after day, her perpetually screwed, coal-black eyes spewing lasers of disdain and loathing.

I don't know why. I had no explanation at the time and I've none to this day. I thought I was a nice guy. She disagreed. I guess you could say she hated me.

No: I don't have to guess. She *hated* me.

She was just a *baahstid*, I guess.

By way of further explanation, she once took an empty box and threw it at my head. Just like that. I was sitting at my desk, working, and she walked up to me, took an empty cardboard box and threw it at my head. Then she glared at me, as if she were expecting some kind of response. I don't know what she thought I might say.

What would *you* say?

Are you understanding any of this?

I didn't think so. And you think you have problems at *your* job?

Her son was just as precious. He was in his twenties, but his parents openly referred to him by his childhood nickname, and one that any five-year-old would be proud to be identified by. He never posted any objection. He probably didn't dare.

He was perpetually angry – furious, really – a smoldering

volcano of a young man, who seemed ready to erupt at any time. I never saw him smile and I didn't think he was capable of doing so. One of his favorite pastimes was sneaking up behind me while I was making copies at the copy machine. He would stand there, breathing heavily down my neck, practically rubbing his body against mine, snorting and fidgeting and pawing at the ground with the tip of his shoe like a mad bull. I could never tell whether he simply objected to me making copies, whether he thought I wasn't making them fast enough, or something else.

Then there was the father; the *crème de la crème* of the clan, so to speak. He was an obese, sadistic, swine of a man with dyed red hair. During meetings, he had the habit of eating Kellogg's Corn Flakes cereal mixed with taco sauce. He considered it diet food.

Now *there's* a product endorsement for you!

One time, I was in his office for a brief chat when one of the nicest students in the school knocked on the door. He was a big kid but a gentle giant and everybody loved him. He had a small complaint – more like a suggestion, really – and he asked to speak to the owner. He was invited into the office and I immediately became concerned. I mean, my boss didn't give a *crap* what *anyone* thought, much less what one of his students thought, and his daily routine didn't include doing anything *normal*, either.

I forget what the kid's small issue was, but I clearly remember that he couldn't have been more polite. Hell, he was the dictionary definition of *courteous*, and he used so many sentences that started with "please" and "sir" that tears began to well up in my eyes. I think I might have adopted him right then and there, I do.

The owner smiled craftily as the young man spoke. Unlike his sorry offspring, he actually smiled frequently, but it was never a good thing when he did. It was more like a portent of *doom*, and it certainly was in this case.

He began to bait the kid; ridiculing him, insulting him and deriding him, over and over again. At first the young man was mystified. Then, he asked him to stop. As the abuse continued, he began to lose his patience. His eyes bulged and his face reddened. Finally, he began to scream.

And, I think, he started to remember he was six-foot-four; that, too.

When he took two steps toward my boss I intervened, and put the entire weight of my intimidating 125 pound frame between the two. I tried to talk the kid down. As I did, I noticed my superior do two things:

First, he removed a switchblade from a drawer and put it on his desk.

Then, he picked up the phone, dialed 911, and reported that a student had attacked him with a knife.

One of his staff was restraining the student, he added.

As stunned as I was, I was more concerned for my enraged charge than for my own sensibilities. I successfully ushered him out of the office and returned to my *room*, shaken to my core.

Soon thereafter I was summoned back to the owner's office. Two policemen were there. "*Dave* will tell you what happened," the owner said to the cops.

I looked at my boss, then at the officers, then at my boss again. Without a word, I turned my back and successfully ushered *myself* out of the office, out of the school, and out of the employment of this monster.

Listen: I'm not making this up. There are really people like this. This is a true story.

OK.

But *none* of this is really what I wish to relate to you. I offer this information only to put my prior conduct into some kind of context.

I neglected to mention that in the *room* I worked in there was an electric coffee pot. It was a very expensive coffee pot, sitting on a small table all by itself, and all day long the family took turns attending to it: cleaning it, adding coffee and water, changing filters and re-stocking all of the necessary *accoutrements* that any sophisticated coffee connoisseur would otherwise require. I'm sure that only the finest coffee beans were employed, imported from exotic and distant lands and at a scandalous price too outrageous to mention. All day I would be tortured with the sumptuous aromas rising continuously from that pot.

Despite the considerable human traffic continually passing through this *room* of mine, it was well known by all that *this* coffee was for the *family* and for no one else. No teacher, no student and no staff member even acknowledged the existence of that pot, or so much as favored it with a glance, as if fearing that if they did they might turn to stone, as if they had looked at Medusa.

I didn't give two craps who worshiped the coffee pot. I wasn't going to revere it as if it were some graven idol, and I wasn't about to give it the respect I would, say, a *chain saw*, either. And while I thoroughly disliked my working conditions, as well as the people I was compelled to work for, after all, I was an assured and confident man. I had a strong sense of self-worth and little insecurity with respect to my thoroughly male personality. I had shoulders broad enough and a temperament even enough to tolerate the strange and aberrant proclivities of the dolts I was surrounded by.

And then, one day, something happened.

My father was in the hospital recovering from heart surgery. It was a big deal and I probably shouldn't have been at work. I was worried about him, and everyone at the school knew I was. Further, I was expecting to hear from him that morning, as soon as he felt well enough to speak, and everyone knew that, too.

Including the bimbo.

The call came in around 11:00 a.m. For some reason it was diverted to her desk, not mine. She picked up the phone and it immediately became clear to me that my father was on the line.

They had a brief conversation. She didn't appear receptive to anything he was saying. She glared at me. Then she slammed the phone into its cradle and went back to work.

Somewhere, deep inside of me, a switch flipped *on*.

I don't know how I got the idea. I'm not sure why I choose the coffee pot, except that it was an object all three of them cherished. It had the advantage of being an inanimate one, as well, and incapable of resisting in any way. Finally, it all seemed a rather efficient use of my time, as I could strike back against the entire family simultaneously.

So, later that day I found myself alone in the room with the coffee pot. I stared fiercely at it and smiled cruelly. I don't know if coffee pots can actually get *frightened* but, I must tell you, this one looked positively *alarmed* and for good reason.

I rose from my desk slowly and walked methodically, step by measured step to the entrance door, closed it softly and locked it. I moved to the pot just yards away. I reminded myself to be careful. I slid the glass carafe out of the apparatus that contained it. I removed the plastic piece that covered it and placed it aside. The pot was full and steam rose freely from the flask.

And then, I spit in the coffee pot.

I spit in the coffee pot and gently swirled the contents until the spit disappeared. I replaced the plastic top, put the carafe back in place, removed myself to the door, unlocked it and left it ajar. Then, I returned to my desk and my work.

And, I waited. I waited for the bimbo to return. Quite patiently, I think.

Sometimes, the smallest things can liberate a man and make him feel like a *man* again. And before you judge me too harshly, please do keep in mind that this incident occurred many years ago, long before feats like this might be considered *unhealthy* or something.

There was a time, you know, when spit was just *spit*.

Anyway, soon thereafter, the door opened and my heart took a leap as it did. I looked up and saw the son standing in the entrance way, both hands on his hips, glaring at me with that impetuous, imperial scowl on his face. He moved to the coffee pot and began to pour himself a cup, turning every moment or so to glower fiercely at me. He was sending me a clear message and it was this:

"Don't even _think_ of drinking this coffee!"

I smiled politely.

I would certainly take his unspoken advice.

At that moment, I didn't think I had ever been happier.

The day passed without further incident. But it was followed by the next day.

They say you can never have enough of a good thing and, in many ways, I think this is true. It was certainly true as pertained to the coffee pot and my sinister designs toward it.

So, bright and early that morning, with adrenaline pumping through my veins and with glee surging through my heart, I began to duplicate the prior day's activities. But this time when I locked the door and turned to the pot, the door handle began to rattle impatiently. Unnerved, I turned and opened the door, ready for anything. Timothy, one of the school's teachers, filled the doorway when I did.

He was an imposing man of Caribbean descent: tall, handsome, soft-spoken and muscled from head to toe. Gratefully, we were friends. And while we were dissimilar in many ways, we did have one thing in common.

We detested them. We detested all three of them.

I had little hesitation disclosing my secret to Timmy and he was fairly delighted to learn of it. In fact, he _insisted_ that he be allowed to participate.

Sometimes it's easy for even a fool like me to realize when he's _on_ to something. Anyway, who was _I_ to turn down the reasonable request of a dear friend?

Besides, it wasn't _my_ friggin' coffee pot.

We locked the door and turned to the pot.

You know what we did. Both of us.

Swirling, swirling.

Timothy was beside himself; he was happy, he really was. He explained that while Lincoln may have freed the slaves long ago, he had never felt *quite* so free as at that moment.

I remained perfectly satisfied with the entire affair.

Timothy *insisted* that we *had* to tell Joseph. Joseph was another teacher. He was very close to Jeri, another teacher. Who was *soooo popular*. As you can imagine, all of these people – aside from being amiable and agreeable individuals – had one other thing in common.

You guessed it.

Hated. Them.

Clearly, what had started out as a modest undertaking designed for my amusement alone had expanded considerably, now apparently conferring considerable benefits to the community at large.

I think you can imagine what happened next.

Inductees were admitted into our club, one by one, by way of a ritual. The senior members would stand facing each other, forming a gauntlet the proposed member was compelled to walk through to make it to the coffee pot, where the sacred task of spitting in the pot was to be performed. All the while, we would clap our hands and quietly chant, *"do it – do it – do it."*

At one point there were eight of us. But one day, by the time everyone got there for the regular initiation of a new enrollee, it was late in the afternoon. Only one coffee cup's worth of Java remained in the pot.

This caused some of our group to hesitate, including me, and for obvious reasons. After all, this was still supposed to be a *clandestine* operation. One simply couldn't permit more spit than coffee to be in the pot. That would be *gauche* and vulgar and obvious and would, in any event, secure *someone's* rapid *dis-em-ployment*. That someone, in all likelihood, being me.

Nonetheless, throwing caution to the winds, we forged on like troopers. After all, we *were* rather dedicated, and there was little question that we had gone *all in* on this *thang* of ours, so to speak.

The *swirling* was not as effective as it normally was in disguising our activities. Much to our chagrin, we discovered that the saliva of eight committed people tended to overwhelm a mere six ounces of coffee, even without the cream and sugar.

In desperation, I grabbed a small handful of pens from a container on the wife's desk. Using these instruments, I stirred the pot rapidly with a determined vigor while trying to remember every one of the cooking shows I'd ever seen for some kind of guidance. Once the task at hand appeared concluded, my crew rapidly disbanded, leaving me alone in the room. I was to be the solitary observer and reporter of whatever would follow. Well, me, along with the coffee pot, and *it* wasn't talking. By this time I'm sure it was thoroughly traumatized.

The wife walked in no more than sixty seconds later, not nearly enough time to allow the sweat to dry from my brow or permit my heart rate to decrease. She hesitated at the doorway, immediately suspicious of *something*, and then moved slowly towards the pot, all the while keeping her eye on me.

I returned to my work.

Well, actually, I stared at the blotter on my desk. I wrote something down. On the back of my hand, I believe. She began to reach for the pot, her demon eyes fixed on me all the while.

She was going to realize something was amiss. After all, by my calculation, the pot contained two parts coffee and one part human spit. What remained was a gray-brown viscous mixture that didn't even *look* like coffee anymore, and appeared better suited to be employed as mortar rather than as a refreshing beverage.

But she wasn't looking at the coffee pot. She glared at me while her practiced hands moved automatically. She reached for the pot, then her favorite green cup, and then poured the liquid into the cup expertly, adding a bit of fresh cream as a finishing touch. She turned to devote her full attention to me as she stirred the tempting brew.

The moment of retribution was at hand, and I decided to get my full dollar's worth of entertainment, which, coincidentally, was about the price of a cup of coffee in those days. I carefully, dramatically placed my papers aside. I took a deep breath. I leaned back in my chair with my hands behind my neck. As she slowly brought the cup to her lips, I smiled broadly.

She stopped in mid-sip.

"What are *you* smiling at?" she barked.

"I don't know, madam, I guess I'm just a happy guy," I replied.

"And why the hell are *you* so happy?" she asked, as she brought the cup to her lips once again.

"I really don't know," I said, choking back laughter.

"I guess I just love *people.*"

Who wants to be a Billionaire?

WE ARE BACK ON THE ISLAND OF ST. MAARTEN, AGAIN, and you shouldn't complain because it's a lovely place for you to be, particularly because I'm not making you pay for it. We were staying at *La Samana,* a venerable hotel located on the French side of the island.

My family was dining at the hotel's stunning restaurant. We were eating early, as is sometimes our preference, and we were enjoying each other, and the food, and our vacation, and the view of a spectacularly beautiful azure sea. The ocean was tranquil that day, as was the restaurant. We were the only ones in the place, except for a woman in her mid-thirties who was dining in solitary fashion, quietly gazing at the sea as she ate.

It was a beautiful spot, and thoroughly romantic, a fact that wasn't lost on either my wife or I. This was despite the vociferous presence of our charming teenage daughters, who are usually inclined to take over any meal, any party, any *things* they engage themselves in or any *places* they tend to be.

Which include, at the present time, the cities of Boston and Miami.

Back to St. Maarten. As boisterous as our table was, the sight of a woman alone in such a dreamy place was unusual, particularly since she seemed so *sad* and so very alone.

All of a sudden she began to cry softly to herself.

I hope I don't flatter myself when I say that I'm a sensitive soul, which may be a funny thing for a lawyer to say. One of a litigator's jobs is to redistribute money from one person to another, while slicing off a hefty portion of those funds for himself in the process. To do this for a living every day requires that a certain part of you become cold and unfeeling, even if you pride yourself on always being on the right side of a case.

But there's another part of you that remains quite human,

and that has to, and I find myself unable to watch a person suffer for very long without trying to do something about it, regardless of whether it will make me money or not.

My wife knows this and I can't say she always approves. She understands the value of altruism, of course, and recognizes that I am often compelled – for personal reasons – to help people when I can. Oftentimes, she has witnessed me thrust myself into a person's life in order to do so. Whether they want me there or not.

Thus, she also knows the meaning of the word *interference*. She has tried to teach me – unsuccessfully, I'm afraid – that sometimes people simply wish to be left alone, and that even kindness can be unwanted now and again.

It can also interrupt your *dining.* As it did on this occasion.

My wife noticed I was distracted by the woman's tears. She sighed. Like my inclination to leave dirty socks on the floor, some of my proclivities have become predictable over the years. Eventually, I could take no more.

"You know I have to do *something*," I said to Andrea, after watching the woman sob for almost twenty minutes.

"I know," she replied.

My girls fell silent, mainly because *something* unusual usually happens when Daddy does *anything*. I think they've come to believe that their father is like a never-ending fairy tale, with a whole bunch of *alternate endings,* many of which tend to be rather entertaining.

I rose from my chair and approached the woman. I asked if I could join her for a moment. I sat down before she could reply.

While I do know a bit about counseling people, you should also know that dabbling with people's minds, or pretending to be a psychiatrist, can be a dangerous thing for both the dabbler and the *dabbleree.* Nevertheless, I asked the woman why she was crying and why she was alone in such a beautiful setting. And she told me.

Her name was Mary Ellen, and she was recently divorced from a man she had met in this restaurant years ago. By her account, it had been a terrible marriage. But St. Maarten had become a special place to her, and she had returned to recapture it for herself, determined that the break-up not ruin her love for the island.

It was a poignant story, filled with courage and with hope, and I was touched. She appeared appreciative of my company, and began to describe her life growing up as an only child in the State of Texas.

Where all that oil comes from.

Where her loving Grandpa, *the oilman,* came from, too.

She described her life as one filled with sadness and where there were few people, except Grandpa, that she felt she could trust.

It was especially difficult, she said, to find a *lawyer* you could trust.

I *so agreed* with that statement.

She went on to tell me how Grandpa had bought up so many of those pesky oilfields littering the State of Texas, and how so *many* of them had become polluted by *oil.* Well, Grandpa just *had* to dispose of them somehow. So he convinced some big oil company to buy up the properties, and he was glad to be rid of them.

He sold the fields for fifty million dollars.

That was in 1940.

"But Grandpa was smart," she added.

"Right?" I thought in my head.

"Really?" I asked.

"Oh yes," she replied. "He made sure that the oil company also agreed to give him a percentage of the profits from all that oil."

"A percentage?" I asked, as innocently as I could.

"Ten percent," she replied.

"For how long?" I inquired, hoping I wasn't prying.

"Forever," she said.

"That long?"

"Yes," she replied. "He had them put the money into a company he bequeathed to his only grandchild."

"His *only* grandchild?" I asked, my heart doing a stutter-step. She smiled demurely.

"It's so difficult to find a lawyer you can trust," she added.

I don't necessarily believe in *chasing* money, folks, but I do believe that money sometimes follows good deeds. And when it does, I think it perfectly consistent with all my charitable convictions and spiritual beliefs to seize as much of it as I can, and as quickly as possible.

I took a deep breath. I truly appreciated this unexpected turn in the conversation.

I wanted to help this woman, I really did. But she was still so distraught: still so damaged, and I had so little left in my mental arsenal that could assist her.

But I did have the *kids*.

I have previously referred to my two daughters as Chaos and Mayhem. This is a description I shall not retreat from now, mainly because they already know that this is what I call them, and by this time take considerable pride from their nicknames. I guess, to them, it's proof positive that they've *accomplished* something. And, moreover, *exactly* what they've set out to achieve since they were infants. Which is to create what I call them.

But, for all of this, they *can* be *amusing*.

Stephanie is just gorgeous, with deep blue eyes and a perfect smile, and she knows had to use all of these things. The sight of her throwing her hair back in exaggerated fashion and employing her considerable weaponry can be arresting. She also gives all the appearance of being *normal*, and can maintain this ruse for some time. But, once she feels she knows you, she quickly reverts to her more natural state, which is abject madness. She becomes wild and unpredictable, liable to do most anything, and she is literally *hysterical*. Meaning only that she's very *funny*.

She's also incredibly *charming* when she wishes to be, just like her younger sister, Ariana, who's as cute as a button and a brilliant conversationalist, and compliments her sister perfectly. Assuming she's in a good mood.

As bent toward destruction and revolution as they often are, my beloved children have also been known to rise to the occasion and did so in this instance.

Without daring to remove my eyes from *my new best friend*, I raised my right hand and beckoned them. They appeared instantly, as bubbly and as bright and as beautiful as I've ever seen them, instinctively sensing their roles in this mission and eagerly prepared to spread the joy of their being throughout the world.

Or at least as far as the State of Texas.

Of course, they couldn't have known about the *black gold*.

Could they?

Well it seemed that they did, because I've never seen my kids so entertaining or so delightful. For an hour they joked and giggled and charmed their way into Mary Ellen's heart. I sat back and played my solitary and silent role as proud parent, until one of them was sitting on her knee, and the other was demonstrating her latest dance routine, much to the delight of their Southwestern belle.

And then, as if on cue, Andrea arrived. She had wisely sat back and allowed her *henchchildren* to soften the mark up. Now she was here to deliver the killer blow. Which she did.

The pair bonded instantly, chatting first about the kids, then the restaurant, then the hotel, then the island, then all of the things on the island. And then about everything else that had ever existed anywhere.

All of a sudden, I realized my family had been collectively yakking for over an hour and a half. I had not said a word in that time and I was getting fidgety. Besides, I'd barely started my appetizer when I decided to call this summit and all this gushing was getting me hungry.

Mary Ellen, our own Texas gusher, obviously delighted with the entire affair and now entirely cured of her depression, suggested that we all come over to her *villa* for lunch the following afternoon. We should all bring our bathing suits. For the *pool* in her *villa*.

Andrea instantly agreed for all of us, fully apprised of the family rules permitting her to do so without checking with me. Or even looking at me.

But I didn't mind. The villa sounded nice. I'd be happy to bring a bathing suit. Hell, I was in pretty good shape, and thought at the time there would be no harm adding a bit of *sex* into the mix if I could.

And I could bring my briefcase along.

As soon as I thought that thought I felt ashamed; I did. But only for a second.

Mary Ellen soon changed her mind. Instead, she decided she would take us all out to dinner the following evening at the finest restaurant on the island.

Of course she would.

Our repast at the hotel restaurant otherwise ended uneventfully.

When we arrived back at our room I seized Stephanie's laptop and told her I was going to do some research on our new *bestest* buddy. The kids – always keenly engrossed by any activity that might generate *cash* without requiring any effort on their part – crowded around me with interest. I keyed in the name of the company Mary Ellen had identified.

It came up instantly, and it was a public company, listed on the NY Stock Exchange. I dug a little further. Only two employees were listed. One was a lawyer. The other was her. I began to sweat profusely.

The business of the company was to collect the profits from oil sales generated by over 1,000 oilfields in the Lone Star State.

There were nineteen million shares of stock in the hands of investors. Shares were selling for over fifty dollars.

I could only interpret this data in one way.

Uhhh, Mary Ellen was a *billionaire*.

The kids sat up at full attention on the bed and looked at each other. They had clearly come to their own conclusions, said conclusions having required their full attention.

I called a family conference and everyone assembled around me.

I know we all had a lot of *fun* with Mary Ellen, I said, but this is not playtime, this is *business*. It didn't start out that way, but that's the way it is now. We're going to a dinner, and Daddy's going to *dominate* that dinner. He's going to be caring and witty, and brilliant, and charming, and *any other frigging thing* he needs to be to secure employment with the billionaire.

This was *Daddy's* dinner. This was *business*. Everyone follows his lead.

That was what I said.

My wife was silent. My daughters nodded their heads obediently. I was satisfied they understood. So we went to dinner.

Le Tastevin is a wonderful restaurant, and I think it's the best on St. Maarten, just as advertised, and I don't mind giving it a plug. It has wonderful food, delightful ambiance and an accommodating management that was *most* happy to see their *favorite billionaire* once again.

As I was. My children were dressed beautifully and came to the place with all of their most potent *adorableness* on full display. Fully prepared, they both winked knowingly to me as they were seated. They were on board. After all, they were expert manipulators in their own right and had little objection to picking up a few tips from the *master*. They also knew that if their daddy was successful tonight, all the cash that was earned from his efforts would ultimately flow to them, if not during *his* lifetime, then almost *certainly* during theirs.

As I said, they were on board.

I said nothing when Ariana's calculator popped out of her purse as she sat down. It was nothing, really; no one noticed at all, and I'd need it soon anyway, along with a dozen empty suitcases to bring all those bearer bonds home with me.

Andrea looked lovely, as well, undoubtedly prepared to play the dutiful and respectful wife, who would look adoringly at her husband for hours, nodding her head wisely in agreement at everything he said.

I need to tell you something about my spouse because it's the right time and I can't keep it in anymore, anyway.

You see, Andrea's a *sociable* type of gal. At first she appears quiet and reserved, and she really is: at least up until the moment someone engages her in conversation. It can be as simple as a mere *hello*. Then, as if a match has been touched to a fuse, everything that follows seems to be determined by some unalterable law of physics even Einstein never anticipated. There's something almost mechanical about what happens to her, and the transformation that takes place never fails to amaze me. She becomes a nuclear-powered *mouth machine* without an off switch.

Yes.

I just answered the question you were thinking in your head.

Yes; Andrea *did* read that line.

No. She didn't like it.

Yes. She asked that it be removed before you could read it.

The gall of some people. My charming spouse had little objection to me making her the most adorable woman on planet Earth for almost three hundred pages – and in *two* of these books, no less – and the minute I say something *truthful...*

Oops.

Anyway, lest you think me disingenuous, I concede that *I* am a mouth machine too, as should be clear to all of you by now, so I'm in a poor position to be judgmental or critical. I've often stated that my mouth first gets me into trouble, and then, gets me out of it.

But, I have an excuse. I make my *living* being a mouth machine. I talk not just for the sheer pleasure of it, but to make money from it. Besides, even *I* know that there's a time to talk, and a time to be silent, and that a failure to distinguish between the two may *cost* me money.

Like, for instance, when a judge says, "...Counselor, if you say *one more word*, I'll..."

You get the picture.

So, I must be disciplined when I speak, as silence can sometimes be just as profitable as verbosity.

Andrea has no such restraint and suffers from none of the disabilities that result from such stilted thinking. Nor has she any interest in my silly theories and would not ascribe to any if she had. She talks because she *can,* and because she enjoys it, and because everyone around her seems to enjoy it when she does.

And she proceeded to on this occasion, from the very moment she was seated, and with remarkable gusto and enthusiasm.

Essentially, her conversation with Mary Ellen just picked up where they'd left it, and she was really entertaining, she was. At least our kind host thought so. They laughed and chortled and chuckled as if they'd known each other all of their lives, as my daughters and I looked on with rank amazement.

An hour into their conversation, with our appetizers still before us, Ariana dropped her fork onto her plate with a loud *clang.* This was her subtle way of saying that maybe her father had the patience for this drivel, but *she* certainly didn't.

"*Shuuuush,*" my wife said with a broad smile on her face, as if Ariana had done something *really droll.* And then, she returned to her conversation.

Ariana, dropping all pretension, flashed my wife a disingenuous and patronizing smile. Then, she summoned the waiter. In a moment our *garcon* was tableside.

"Yes, Miss?" he dutifully inquired.

Ariana smiled politely.

"What's the legal drinking age in St. Maarten?" she asked.

"It's eighteen, Miss," he replied with some hesitation.

"Is it?" she asked.

"Yes," he replied.

"That high?"

"Unfortunately," he said.

"Never mind then," she concluded. She turned her head in dramatic fashion and flashed her mother the most condescending sneer I've ever seen.

"That's *hysterical!*" Mary Ellen gasped between fits of laughter.

"Never mind *her*," my betrothed responded gleefully. "*Let me tell you about the time...*"

"*Mommy is blowing the billions*," Stephanie mouthed silently to me, shock painted all over her face.

I tried to speak and found I couldn't, primarily because I needed air in my lungs to do so. Most of it had left there some time ago. My jaw dropped open and stayed that way.

Ariana glared at me and snarled. After a moment, I realized she couldn't *possibly* be mad at *me*. She was just communicating telepathically, as a father and daughter are able to do now and again.

I tried to drink what was left of my third rum and found I couldn't. I had to be able to close my lips to accomplish this, and *that* wasn't going to happen anytime soon. I placed my glass back down on the table and concentrated, trying to pick up my loving daughter's thoughts.

She was telling me I *still* had to pay for college.

Something like the last breath of a dying man escaped my lips.

Then I got my second wind, so to speak. If *I* was going to go down, I was going to go down fighting. Or more accurately, *talking*.

I straightened my back along with my tie and stretched my neck like a prizefighter waiting for the final round in a bout. I began to actually *listen* to the pair's mindless claptrap, which had earlier taken on all the coherence of a conversation between insects. I waited politely for an opportunity to interject a word or two and found it.

It was only a brilliant witticism followed by a terse one-liner and ably delivered, if I do say so myself, but for some reason I was still surprised at the response.

"*Shuuuush,*" my wife said, still smiling, but not even favoring me with a glance. She waved me off with a dismissive gesture as if I were an infant that had just attempted language for the first time. The rhythm of her ongoing exchange was barely interrupted.

Well, I wouldn't try *that* again.

We all suffered through the rest of the meal – except Andrea and Mary Ellen, that is, who enjoyed themselves *immensely* – and it lasted all of three hours. I smiled weakly at our host at the end of the evening and thanked her for a lovely dinner. She flashed a pixie-like smile. Then she asked me why *wonderful* women like Andrea always seem to marry some lawyer.

I think it was a rhetorical question.

We sat in our rented Jeep outside of the restaurant. All of us were in shock, I think. Except Andrea, who was still quite the *bubbly broad.*

"Daddy, I don't think she gets it," Ariana offered.

I looked at Stephanie. She was staring at me, shaking her head back and forth rapidly, hugging herself, unable to speak, but still able to express the fact that all of this had *really freaked her out.*

My wife was oblivious, adjusting herself demurely for the ride home.

As my vocal cords were fully rested by that time, and as all the artificial restraints placed upon them seemed to have been lifted when we left the restaurant, I decided to test the waters and verbalize a bit.

"Do you know what you just did?" I asked my wife. It seemed like a fair question at the time.

"What?" she inquired, and quite innocently, smiling brilliantly as she did.

"Mommy, you talked for *three hours!*" Stephanie blurted out, somewhat exasperated.

"You wouldn't...shut the...**** up..." Ariana added, never one to mince words, and emphasizing each so there would be little doubt as to her meaning.

"Do you know what you just did?" I asked again. I wasn't sure why I repeated myself, but it was possible that because I hadn't spoken in such a long time, I'd simply forgotten many of the words in the English language.

It took a while before she could be made to understand, and it took all three of us to explain it to her. But she eventually realized that the price of her evening's entertainment had been *food and shelter for the next thirty years.*

She became rather contrite. We spoke little of the episode in the years that followed.

There is a happy moral to this tale, Dear Readers, do not fear: and rest assured it has *nothing* to do with that old adage, *silence is golden.*

It's true that I believe we should all be rewarded for our good works, and not only in the next life, but in this one, as well. It's not that we should expect a payment for our compassion, or seek a cash prize in exchange for our decency. We cannot, as T. S. Elliot proscribed, do the right deed for the wrong reason. It's just that I would like to think that in a properly functioning universe people who do good things will have good things returned to them.

The thing is, the universe doesn't always function properly. Much like a poodle or a teenager, it often does what it wishes to do. And when it does, perhaps it is then that the best laid schemes of Mice and Men go awry, as Robert Burns said, and leave us with nothing but grief for promised joy, as appears to have occurred in the case at bar.

Or maybe we just have the wrong idea of what *joy* is and where it really comes from.

Andrea has some very specific feelings in this regard. You see, she's never read Mr. Burns and cares not two hoots for whether the universe is functioning or not, because her happiness doesn't depend on anything the universe does.

She doesn't think that joy comes from anywhere or results from anything in particular. She doesn't think you have to scheme, plot or plan for it to happen. She thinks you can just create it with nothing at all, out of thin air, anytime you wish, or find it anywhere you choose to look for it.

She believes that even a road leading to disappointment can delight and amaze along the way, and that a measure of bliss can be extracted from even the harshest failure.

She thinks that three hours of fun and laughter can never produce anything *bad*. It can only produce *joy*, and that's really the *point* of all this, isn't it?

That's what she thinks.

It's a wonderful way to live.

It can be elusive, this thing called *happiness*. It can be difficult to grasp, like trying to seize a fistful of water from a pond. We can't barter for it or purchase it with a credit card and all of our good fortune may not be sufficient to secure it. We tend to think of it as a destination of some kind, as a place we could reach if only we traveled a certain road long and far enough. But it's not.

I have come to believe that happiness is something that each of us can find. It doesn't make a difference what road we travel upon, and it doesn't even make a difference where we ultimately wind up.

And we don't have to look very far. We can find it anywhere

along the way. Because it's not on the road at all, not really.

It's within all of us. It was all the time.

It is right now.

That's the best I got.

Thanks for reading.

- THE END -

Other books by David I. Aboulafia:
Snapshots From My Uneventful Life
Roundfire Books
ISBN: 978-1-78099-292-1 (2d Edition, 2017)

Visions Through a Glass, Darkly
Cosmic Egg Books
ISBN: 978-1-78535-022-1 (2016)

Correspondence to the author can be addressed to:
228 East 45th Street, Suite 1700
New York, NY 10017

Roundfire

FICTION

Put simply, we publish great stories. Whether it's literary or popular, a gentle tale or a pulsating thriller, the connecting theme in all Roundfire fiction titles is that once you pick them up you won't want to put them down.
If you have enjoyed this book, why not tell other readers by posting a review on your preferred book site. Recent bestsellers from Roundfire are:

The Bookseller's Sonnets
Andi Rosenthal
The Bookseller's Sonnets intertwines three love stories with a tale of religious identity and mystery spanning five hundred years and three countries.
Paperback: 978-1-84694-342-3 ebook: 978-184694-626-4

Birds of the Nile
An Egyptian Adventure
N.E. David
Ex-diplomat Michael Blake wanted a quiet birding trip up the Nile – he wasn't expecting a revolution.
Paperback: 978-1-78279-158-4 ebook: 978-1-78279-157-7

Blood Profit$
The Lithium Conspiracy
J. Victor Tomaszek, James N. Patrick, Sr.
The blood of the many for the profits of the few... *Blood Profit$*
will take you into the cigar-smoke-filled room where American
policy and laws are really made.
Paperback: 978-1-78279-483-7 ebook: 978-1-78279-277-2

The Burden
A Family Saga
N.E. David
Frank will do anything to keep his mother and father apart. But
he's carrying baggage – and it might just weigh him down ...
Paperback: 978-1-78279-936-8 ebook: 978-1-78279-937-5

The Cause
Roderick Vincent
The second American Revolution will be a fire lit from an
internal spark.
Paperback: 978-1-78279-763-0 ebook: 978-1-78279-762-3

Don't Drink and Fly
The Story of Bernice O'Hanlon: Part One
Cathie Devitt
Bernice is a witch living in Glasgow. She loses her way in her
life and wanders off the beaten track looking for the garden of
enlightenment.
Paperback: 978-1-78279-016-7 ebook: 978-1-78279-015-0

Gag
Melissa Unger

One rainy afternoon in a Brooklyn diner, Peter Howland punctures an egg with his fork. Repulsed, Peter pushes the plate away and never eats again.
Paperback: 978-1-78279-564-3 ebook: 978-1-78279-563-6

The Master Yeshua
The Undiscovered Gospel of Joseph
Joyce Luck

Jesus is not who you think he is. The year is 75 CE. Joseph ben Jude is frail and ailing, but he has a prophecy to fulfil ...
Paperback: 978-1-78279-974-0 ebook: 978-1-78279-975-7

On the Far Side, There's a Boy
Paula Coston

Martine Haslett, a thirty-something 1980s woman, plays hard on the fringes of the London drag club scene until one night which prompts her to sign up to a charity. She writes to a young Sri Lankan boy, with consequences far and long.
Paperback: 978-1-78279-574-2 ebook: 978-1-78279-573-5

Tuareg
Alberto Vazquez-Figueroa

With over 5 million copies sold worldwide, *Tuareg* is a classic adventure story from best-selling author Alberto Vazquez-Figueroa, about honour, revenge and a clash of cultures.
Paperback: 978-1-84694-192-4

Readers of ebooks can buy or view any of these bestsellers by clicking on the live link in the title. Most titles are published in paperback and as an ebook. Paperbacks are available in traditional bookshops. Both print and ebook formats are available online.

Find more titles and sign up to our readers' newsletter at
http://www.johnhuntpublishing.com/fiction

Follow us on Facebook at
https://www.facebook.com/JHPfiction
and Twitter at https://twitter.com/JHPFiction